$1 50
2|22

A Penny For Luck

Voodoo Rumors 1951

A Penny For Luck

Voodoo Rumors 1951

By D. Alan Lewis

A Penny For Luck
Voodoo Rumors 1951

Published by D. Alan Lewis and
Voodoo Rumors Media

Interior and Cover by D. Alan Lewis
Edited by Dana Fraedrich

Voodoo Rumors Media
Nashville, Tennessee 37211

Acknowledgements

Many thanks to my editor, Dana Fraedrich and all my beta readers. Special thanks to David Ramey for all his efforts to keep my websites up and running.

In addition, a big thanks to my kids for keeping me on my toes.

One

I awoke to the scent of honey, flowers, and sex.

Long raven curls framed the round face of a sleeping angel nestled next to me. Not moving for a long while, I studied her with my mouth hung open in awe. Every detail of this woman appeared perfect, as if sculpted by God Himself. Her beauty, the rich full lips, the soft East Indian features, and pale sepia complexion simply could not be measured or entirely appreciated in the span of minutes or even years.

On the other side of this sleeping beauty lay my blonde goddess, Natalie. Her face looked so peaceful, so content, as she rested with an arm draped over the stunning Indian. Two women, just as perfect and beautiful in their own way, graced my bed, and yet appeared as complete opposites in appearance. Sighing at the vision before me, I couldn't for the life of me, remember how we'd all gotten here. I didn't feel surprised by the Indian's presence. Instead, something about her felt familiar, as if I expected her to be here when I awoke.

The stabbing pain started the moment I tried to lift my head too quickly. For a brief moment, I wished for death, but as the pain subsided, I carefully and slowly tried again. Moving with care, I tried not to wake the two nude angels or cause undue pain to reappear within my skull. I rolled to the side of the bed, planted my feet on the floor, and pushed myself up. Bones creaked and popped in the process.

"You're getting old," I muttered to myself, lifting arms to stretch.

Forty isn't really old, unless you're looking at it from your twenties. The wear and tear of four decades, living life hard, and only slowing down during those bad patches when the bottle was my only friend, the painful effects of all that and more shot through my nerves and straight into my brain.

Turning, my eyes feasted on the sight before me. As much as I loved what I saw, there were questions. Looking around the room, a rush of familiarity washed over me. I knew where I stood: room 324 of the Hotel Tennessee. Glancing over my shoulder, the morning sun blazed, filling the sky with vibrant yellow and orange hues. Its light washed over the Memphis skyline, creating glowing lines along the edges of some buildings and almost solid black shadows on others.

Stepping around the bed, I almost tripped over my wadded-up pants. My clothes along with the ladies', littered the floor, lying in a broken line from the door to the bed. I chuckled lightly as I thought about what must have happened. Natalie had joked about experimenting, sexually. Although I didn't remember any of it, we'd obviously not wasted any time getting right to things.

Stealing another look at them from this side of the bed, I sighed in displeasure. Not at the view, but at the fact I wasn't lying there, close to Natalie, with my arm draped over her. The perfect curves of her backside and the seductive form of our guest made me reconsider getting out of bed. Images of climbing back in and pulling them close made me smile.

But who was this unknown vision that graced our presence? Slowly shaking my head, I tried to remember the night before, but each attempt only brought broken images of dancing, drinking, and a smoke-filled bar. Looking back to the clothing, I studied her dress. An elegant red number, long and flowing, trimmed in gold with long sleeves and a low-cut neckline. The mental picture of her wearing it brought a smile to my mug but seeing the garment didn't stir up any memories as I'd hoped. I may have an overly developed thirst for booze, but Natalie usually kept her drinking to a minimum. I could see myself getting sloshed enough to end up in this position; it'd happened too many times before. I lingered for a moment on what Natalie's response to waking up with another woman in the bed would be.

I turned as someone tapped once on and then slipped a card under the room's door. The cream-colored card had an embossed letter 'B' on the front. Bending over to snatch it up felt like a nightmare as the blood rushed up into my head, sending waves of pain and dizziness. Standing upright again helped, but I needed a moment for my senses to return. And coffee. Oh, dear Lord, I needed coffee in the worst way.

After the room stopped spinning, I studied and read the card with burning, blood-shot eyes.

Your presence is required in the Tennessean Bar, located in the hotel's lobby at 8:30. I'll be sitting in the same seat I occupied last night when we spoke. I'm certain your memories of last night have been robbed or heavily blurred by the exuberant amount of alcohol you and your companions consumed before retiring to your bed, but I'll do my best to help you remember our arrangement.

B

P.S.   And please get dressed before leaving your room.

Looking up, I saw the clock read 7:50. I thought about the time and judged that I could make that deadline. Shower, shave, and dress. Rubbing my burning eyes, I read the card again.

"Who the hell is B? And how does he know about the girls? And..." I whispered to no one in particular before looking down at my naked self. "And yep. I need to get dressed. Wouldn't want to scare anyone like this."

Two

The elevator's door hissed open, and I strolled out into the hotel's opulent lobby. The Hotel Tennessee's reputation as one of the South's premiere establishments was well deserved. After checking in the day before, Natalie and I had treated ourselves to a night on Beale Street, hitting the clubs and dancing and drinking like there was no tomorrow.

A young bellhop sitting on a bench near the elevator door jumped to his feet, nodding. I returned the gesture, but I didn't take my eyes off him. Something about him seemed familiar. Had he helped me or Natalie yesterday? Had he taken the bags up when we first got here?

"Looking sharp, sir." He smiled.

"Thanks, kid," I responded, sounding as dreary

and dead as I felt. Glancing down at my suit did perk me up a bit. A light-blue jacket with matching pants and a crisp white shirt. Natalie had insisted on handpicking a pair of new suits and accessories before the trip. She lived by the credo that looking good was halfway to feeling good. Fashion wasn't my strong point, but I'd promised to try and improve my wardrobe choices for her.

Since we'd started this relationship, she'd found plenty of little ways of making my life better. She gave me a reason to take care of myself, instead of staying on the self-destructive course I'd clung to since my wife had passed. Natalie made sure I was eating better, or at least eating a meal instead of getting my nourishment from a whiskey bottle.

Workwise, the P.I. business was making money for a change, meaning she was collecting the income and putting it in the bank, keeping the books updated, and had turned out to be a fairly decent accountant. The fashion bit was the latest attempt to bring me into the 1950's, as she put it.

"Which way is the bar?" I asked.

The bellhop pointed and gave a practiced smile.

Moments later, I stopped and stood in the doorway. A ribbon of cigarette smoke rose from the ashtray in front of the lone figure in the establishment. Perched on a stool at the bar, the man never looked around. Blond and dressed in a white suit, he held a glass out in front of him, taking a couple of slow sips as I approached. Moving up behind him, I watched as he twirled the amber liquid in the curved tumbler and watched it swirl.

"There was a contest many, many years ago," he said in a gravelly voice that sounded like he'd smoked one too many cartons of Camel Unfiltereds.

I glanced around to make sure he wasn't directing the conversation to someone else.

"John Jameson and a friend of mine named Barbas, a thug and badass demon from one of the inner rings, had a wager. Seems that Barbas thought he could out-do Jameson when it came to making a top-notch whiskey."

He took a long sip and let out a contented sigh as I took a seat next to him.

"They both brewed up their concoctions, gave themselves plenty of time, a decade if I remember right, to let their drinks age suitably, and then a dozen townsfolks were chosen to judge and declare a winner."

"You saying you were there?" I asked, watching him nod in response to my query. I huffed, letting him know I thought he was full of shit.

He never looked over at me but kept talking, as if

his conversation was with the remainder of his drink.

"There? Hell, I put on a disguise and wormed my way onto the judges' panel."

I studied the man, finding him familiar and unsettling at the same time. "How'd that go over for them?"

The man turned his head and smiled at me. The image of his weathered face, subtly criss-crossed with faint wrinkles, came back to me. I'd been here before, in this seat, beside him. I knew the voice and his mannerisms.

He held up the glass and chuckled. "Ol' Johnny could stir up the finest back then and his descendants still do today." Up ending the glass, he swallowed the remainder of the amber liquid. "Johnny kept his soul and Barbas lost."

"What'd Johnny win?"

"Immortality."

When I cocked an eyebrow, he chuckled again and continued.

"Not like never-ending life or any of that nonsense. No, no… he won immortality for his personal claim to fame, his finest drink. Immortal success for his business, one that'll last for centuries beyond Ol' Johnny's death. Most men don't want to live forever, not really. What they really want is to be remembered. They want that eternal fame, undying remembrance that so few have been graced with over the course of history."

A lump formed in my throat. "Who are you and why did you ask me to meet you?"

"Don't remember? No, of course you don't." He waved the bartender over. "Get my friend a drink, mix it up like this…"

He tapped his fingers on the counter as if trying to remember. "Equal measures of Jack No.7, Efe Klasik Turkish Raki, and grain alcohol, and stir in a splash of peppermint oil. Oh, and a refill here please." He lifted his own glass in a mock toast.

"Sounds…," I started to say "terrible" but the more I thought about the weird mix of flavors, the more I wanted to see how they'd combine. "Well, actually that sounds pretty interesting."

"You'll need to drink it all." He gave me a wink and tapped his temple. "It'll wake up the brain. Now, you asked a question. My name is rather difficult for most people outside of Ancient Egypt to pronounce, so just call me Barkley."

"What about modern-day Egypt?"

He shrugged. "Wouldn't be easy for them either."

"So, you're Egyptian? Sorry but you don't look the part. With the blond hair and the build, I'd say Scandinavian."

He glanced over at me with a look of annoyance

in his eyes. "You don't look like the kind of man who could fight and beat a mountain-sized behemoth, but we're all full of surprises, aren't we?" He paused and looked longingly at his empty glass. "Let's say I spent some time, let's say a few centuries, near Cairo, a long time ago but I'm originally from—elsewhere."

Moments later, the bartender set a glass in front of me, giving the man next to me a side glance. I could see the look of confusion he had. Like him, I wasn't sure what I was going to be drinking, exactly. My hand reached for the glass when Barkley stopped me.

"Hold on," He said and pulled a small vial from inside his jacket. The fluid in it was clear, and he poured a small amount into the already potent mixture.

"What's that?" I asked, reluctantly lifting the glass and sniffing the drink.

"Holy water." He smirked. "When you're as evil as we are, it gives it a little extra burn on the way down."

"I'm not the evil one here."

He scoffed, "That's a debate we don't have time for this morning."

With his drink refilled, we tapped glasses and I took a small sip to gauge the taste and strength of the concoction. My stomach didn't care for what hit it, and I almost threw it back up.

"Thomas be a man and down it. Just a quick swallow. It'll help."

His words didn't help my mood.

He reached over and placed a hand on my arm. "I need you levelheaded and at your best. Why would I give you a drink to make you ill?"

Breathing deep, I downed that liquid and managed to keep things down. After a moment, all seemed well with the world. My joints moved and flexed without popping, my head was clear, and my eyes didn't burn. More importantly, the hazy memories of last night started clearing. Like pieces of a jigsaw puzzle, random bits of conversations and images started falling into place to show me the whole picture.

He pointed to a booth on the far side of the room. "She sat over there, remember?"

I looked. I did remember the raven-haired Indian bombshell, sitting alone, sipping a drink, and giving no one a bit of notice. After a night of dancing with Natalie, I'd been exhausted and needed a quick rest and a drink or two to recharge.

Natalie felt a little different. Maybe it's her youthful age, but the girl was ready for more.

"You sat here beside me with your girl cuddled up dangerously close and all but grinding against your leg." He sipped at his drink and looked as if he wanted me to continue the story for him.

"You introduced yourself and said you were a record producer. You were here to listen to your new, up and comer perform." It sounded right, but I struggled to make sense of all the splintered memories.

His words took on a menacing tone. "Yes. Exactly the kind of profession that'd grab your young lady's attention. When I asked if you'd like to meet her, you were happy to. Natalie, it seems, took one look and all but dragged us both to the booth. I made introductions, and we talked well into the night."

My eyes followed a path from the bar to the booth, and I remembered the three of us leaving the bar and walking.

"Her name was Anavash. She and Natalie hit it off, talking and laughing." I whispered, and the events played out in my thoughts.

"And?" he asked, his eyes focused on his drink.

I looked at him and then to the stage. "Anavash took to the stage, sang a couple of songs. I remember—I can hear the songs. Her voice was mesmerizing."

"And?"

I couldn't help but smile as I remembered Natalie being called up to the stage by Anavash. She looked perfectly at home, in her element under the spotlight.

"They sang together. Three songs before the show

was over."

"Natalie has a beautiful voice. Remarkable, actually. Their voices really complimented each other," he said as the bartender refilled his glass again.

"Natalie came back to the booth as Anavash sang a couple of more tunes as part of her encore."

Barkley nodded to the side of the booth where Natalie had sat and leaned up against me, happy, content, and exhausted by her performance.

"And your young lady was consumed with excitement and lust. Anavash has that effect on people, but especially Natalie that evening." He chuckled, "The poor girl—Natalie never knew what hit her."

"What are you talking about?" I asked, confused.

Grinning, he answered. "I said something to the likes of, 'even a sane man would sell his soul for a night with her'."

My mouth dropped as I remembered her words through the alcohol-induced haze. The way she looked at the woman, mesmerized, with a look of primal lust in her eyes. Those words she didn't know held any power and that I'd been too drunk and distracted to warn her about.

God. Thomas, look at her. I'd sell my soul for a night with a goddess like her.

I knew Natalie had a certain attraction for other women, an attraction that only seemed to have increased after meeting my sister, Lily, and her vampiric dancers at Voodoo Rumors. But prior to last night, she'd only joked about bringing another woman to join us in the bedroom.

"I told her I had connections in Nashville with various recording studios that I deal with. I happened to have a contract in my pocket, which she gladly signed, giving herself to me. Well, it isn't spelled out in those exact words, but while she thought she was getting a recording contract, I was getting possession of her soul. We signed the papers and shook hands. I snapped my fingers, and then our Indian friend came down from the stage and took my seat as I stepped away. The three of you had another round, and then you and your girl and…"

I swallowed hard. "We went upstairs and…"

Barkley chuckled. "And you had a night of unbridled lovemaking. No, perhaps that isn't the right way of saying it. Lovemaking requires love. What Natalie had for that woman would be considered more of an all-consuming lust. You, of course, were drunk, happy, and had what every man dreams of."

"I get the point." I snarled. "So, what are you saying? You're not Lucifer?"

"No, no. I am merely an associate of the Dark

Lord. One of the originals, but I'm well within my rights to parley on his behalf."

Pulling a pack of cigarettes from his pocket, he offered me one before placing another in his mouth and lighting up. Thing is, he didn't use a match. Instead, a small flame just appeared from the tip of his finger.

Barkley inhaled and let the smoke boil out of his mouth. "The first draw of a freshly lit cigarette is like Heaven on Earth."

I shot him an angry look. "What would you know of Heaven? You're a demon."

He remained calm. "I told you, I'm an original. You know damn well what I am, one of the thirteen that fell. Well, pushed would be more like it. I do remember what it was like up there, all the wonders of Heaven. It is a paradise full of pleasures. But..."

He pulled the cigarette from his mouth and studied it. "But it is so lacking at the same time. None of the things, like these little vices you humans enjoy so much, exist there. Smokes, drinks, sex, none of those are in the Father's realm. Life in paradise glows with wonder and amazement, the likes of which you can't possibly imagine, while at the same time being mind-numbingly dull."

This guy was starting to annoy me. I quickly replayed the events from last night, and something didn't add up. I had a suspicious thought.

My tone grew harsh. "So, you had to wait until we were drunk enough and then throw a hottie at Natalie, in order to trick her in to a deal for her soul. Or did you have to resort to magic tricks too?"

Barkley looked around and smiled. "No, magic wasn't used on you. I wanted your youthful lady friend targeted. Her soul is mine to give to my Lord or to bargain with."

"What does this have to do with her? What happens if I get up and walk out of here? Natalie and I are heading to New Orleans for a vacation. Memphis was just the first stop. No reason to hang around and be bored by you."

I had no intention of leaving until this was resolved but I wanted him to hurry up and get to the point.

He leaned forward, obviously irritated. "You want to make this about the woman. It isn't. This is all about my Boss messing with you and me getting what I need."

Sitting up straight, he waved a hand to the door. "You can go anytime you want. I'm not keeping you here in any way. Just understand, we own her soul, meaning we affect you in a round-about way. When she dies, her soul goes straight to Hell, to serve in whatever way my Master desires. Until then, you're both free to live as you please."

Narrowing my eyes, I growled as I spoke. "Why should I believe any of this shit? First rule in my line of work, never trust anything a demon says."

A hand touched my shoulder, and I spun to see a woman standing behind me. Anavash's smile lit up the room, and her eyes sparkled in a way that immediately had me on my guard.

Barkley smiled warmly. "She's one of our girls."

I watched her nod, and my heart dropped a foot within my chest. The realization of what she really was hit me hard, and I wasn't sure if I was angrier at Barkley for setting this all up or myself for not seeing through the scheme.

"Anavash is a succubus, you see. One of the little tricks she can do is to look deep into your mind to find those aspects of women that you, or in this case, Natalie finds most appealing. In other words, she can make herself into the perfect woman for you or anyone. A woman you simply can't resist, that you can't deny."

Anavash tilted her head as she spoke. Her East Indian accent gave her voice a lyrical quality, as if she almost sang the words. "In Natalie's dreams, I could see an Indian actress, someone she'd seen years ago. A woman that she envisioned as the perfection of beauty and sexuality. Then, I looked into her fantasies and saw the woman she most wanted to encounter, combined those and became the woman you see before you."

I looked at Barkley, "Why not just make Natalie do what you wanted her to do, instead of using all these tricks?"

He looked annoyed and turned to the yell at the barkeep. "My boy, that drink I had you mix for my friend, make a second." He turned back to me. "Like I said, I need you at the top of your game. That question tells me your engine isn't firing on all cylinders. Another drink should remove the remaining clouds from your head."

Anavash giggled as she spoke. "Silly Thomas. Demons can't make humans do anything like that. We can only tempt them into doing what we want. Whisper naughty suggestion or fire up their lust or their anger and rage"

"Only a full-blown possession can accomplish what you're talking about. But the process takes months, sometimes years to groom a human into the state where we can slip inside and wear them like a suit," Barkley remarked.

I took a deep breath and looked at her. "So, this isn't really you?"

She turned on her heels. It was as if the whole of reality shifted in that one instant, moving to the side and realigning. Instead of the beautiful brunette who'd graced my sheets just a little while ago, a demon stood before me. All traces of her East Indian-self had faded away. She was just as beautiful, only with dark reddish skin and flowing raven hair, and a pointed tail that swished around behind her. The red dress had been replaced with one as black as pitch. If she'd had wings and a turned-up nose, she'd have been a double for my sister, Lily.

Barkley saluted her with his cigarette, catching my attention. "Thank you, my love. Now, scamper on home. I'll be along in a while."

When I looked back, she'd disappeared.

"So, now what?" I whispered.

My heart beat faster. The realization of what had happened came crashing down on me. Natalie's soul belonged to Lucifer. I knew I could walk out. Like he said, we could live our lives. The end would come eventually though, and I didn't like the idea of her heading south when she kicked the bucket.

Barkley seemed to sense my despair. "So sad that she places so little value on her own dominion. I'm a little surprised you've not cautioned her on the dangers of casual comments about the ownership of one's soul. I guess moving forward, you'll both choose your words a little more carefully, and think about who you say them too, hmm?"

Part of me wanted to grab the old man and chuck him across the room, demonic nature be damned. Then something he said made the mental gears spin.

I spoke slowly. "You have her soul, but you want to torment me. Why are you still here?"

I watched Barkley's lips twitch.

"You could have left me alone and collected on the deal when she dies, but you called me down here for a reason, didn't you?"

A sly grin appeared, and he tilted his head slightly. "You're not as dumb as I was told. Good. But to answer your question, yes. I do have a deal for you, a wager that could win Natalie's soul back."

"Go on."

"The demon I spoke of earlier, Barbas. He has lost track of something, a very special item, and I need you to retrieve it."

I scoffed. "Simple as that? What's the catch?"

His eyes narrowed, and he smacked his lips, showing a deep annoyance. I loved it. Being tricked and endangering Natalie wasn't the best way to get on my good side.

"Ever hear of Robert Johnson's deal at the Crossroads?" he asked.

I nodded. "He made a deal with the Devil."

"It was never the Devil that made the infamous deal, but one of his proxies."

"Barbas," I muttered.

"Barbas cut a deal with Johnson. It wasn't for riches and fame like the stories say, but for good luck. In the right hands, that'll bring all the fame and fortune a man could ever use. Johnson knew enough to see that fame is fleeting, but good luck would give him a long-lasting career, even when the times changed, and his music fell out of favor. The lucky charm came in the form of a special penny. As long as Johnson kept the coin, all the luck he'd ever need would be on his side. And you know what? It paid off."

I gave a curt nod. "It worked?"

"How do you swinging cats in Nashville say it? 'All the money, booze, and bitches were his for the taking'. Thing is, though, he got careless sometime back. Got a little too drunk and enamored with a pretty face, and he gave the penny away. Since then, the penny has passed through a number of hands."

"So? Just let the next guys have some luck."

"The deal was originally just for Johnson. Letting everyone else benefit from the coin's power, well... let's just say that my Lord wouldn't be happy if he knew about these folks getting all that good fortune without paying for it."

"Finding a penny out in the big wide world is like finding a needle in a haystack. How the hell do you think I'm going to do that?" I asked.

"I spoke to Johnson after his last night on Earth. He gave it to a friend before his death, who gave it to another friend. That last one was in town recently and told me where it is now. Seems it may still be in the hands of a young woman named Margo. She dances at a club called The Golden Rhino. Seems the girl put on a hell of a performance and got a great tip, a coin that'll open doors and put her on the right track to riches and happiness, assuming she uses it the right way."

"Okay, let me get this straight. I follow up on your lead, find this woman, Margo, and get your precious penny back, and then you'll return Natalie's soul?"

"Something like that. We'll remove the mortgage on Miss Natalie's eternal spirit and only collect on it should Saint Peter decide her actions demand a descent."

"Why don't you just go and get it from her? You've already done the leg work and talked to all the people who've had it."

He lifted a cigarette and took a look draw. As the smoke jetted from his nostrils, he spoke. "No. You don't understand. I don't dirty my hands like that. Not unless it is absolutely necessary. Besides, no one I spoke with was on Earth."

I couldn't help but narrow my eyes at the meaning. "They were dead?"

A grin appeared as he responded. "I was right beside them when they died. Talked them up and found out what I needed to know before they even knew if they were going up or down. And for the record, none of them went up."

"You knew when they were going to die?" I asked.

"My boy, it is a long story, and I don't think you've got the ability to truly understand it. Let's just say that yes, I knew when they were going to die," he said. I cocked an eyebrow and waited until he continued. "I didn't kill them. I may be a demon now, but I was originally an angel. And like God, I can exist outside of what you call time. I spoke to them shortly after they died, even though for some, death is years off."

Strangely, I understood the concept, mostly.

"And if I fail?"

He turned the full fury of his dead eyes onto me, then checked his watch. "If you fail, I take the note on her soul and I hand it over to my Lord. Midnight tonight is, as they say, your deadline. Natalie is free to live out her life without any interference from us but once she dies, she will join me for a trip to the second ring, you know, the one dedicated to lust.

She'll be conditioned to serve and put to work taking care of all those horny demons."

"You're a sick bastard, you know that?" I hissed through gritted teeth. "You don't get to touch her."

Barkley smirked. "Only if you choose not to take the challenge. If you do accept the wager, your failure will have consequences. You'll have to live knowing you've failed her."

My anger at the suggestion of using Natalie as a poker chip in his twisted game of chance couldn't be missed, and his nonchalant reaction did little to settle me down.

He rolled his eyes. "My boy, you don't have a choice. Given your lifestyle choices, you and your girl are destined for Hell anyway. Sooner or later, one way or another, that's where sweet Natalie Knight is heading. Since the coin's return is important to me, I'll add this to the pot. You return the penny and I'll see to it that she is exiled back to Earth in the afterlife instead of an eternity of suffering in the fires of Hell. And for good measure, I still have contacts in Heaven and will put in a good word for her. Maybe. Maybe if she stops trying to live up to your example, she can actually get into Heaven."

I bit my lip, mulling over the offer. The terms didn't sit well with me, but he had a point, I don't think either of us were Heaven-bound in the afterlife.

If I could save her soul, they'd provide Natalie with an afterlife, free of hellfire.

"I don't have all day," Barkley said, and he looked at his watch again. "And your time is counting down. It's 9am now. I'll expect you to return the penny at midnight this evening, here in this exact spot."

I hesitated, thinking over the details.

"You said she was asleep. That isn't going to work for me. I need her help and besides, this is as much about her as it is me," I argued.

"Your lady will remain asleep. This is all about you, Thomas. My Lord would love to see you having to live with the guilt of failure. Knowing that every day when you look your lady in the eyes, you'll feel the pangs of regret that you lost her soul to me."

"Your lady? You keep making remarks like that about her. She isn't property. She isn't my property or anyone else's." My anger seeped into the words.

He sighed and shook his head. "I hate this century and its so-called feminism. I preferred a time when a man could trade women as easily as he could trade cattle for goods or property."

I considered punching him but refrained. "Yes, how awful to be you. How long do you think it will it be before Lilith demands equal billing on Hell's marquee?"

He tapped the face of his watch, silently asking the question again.

"I'll agree to the wager, but I'll need everything you know about this Margo and the club she works at. I need more information on the penny. Was it a certain type or year? Identifying markings on it? You'll tell me all you know about it, if I shake on the deal?"

Barkley cocked an eye brow and gave me a crooked smile.

Sneering, I continued. "You gave a first name and the name of a strip club. In my line of work, that's pretty damn thin. This is as much about you getting your coin back as it is for me to get Natalie's soul back. So, if you want to humiliate Barbas, I'll expect you to cooperate."

"I'll tell you what I know."

Not seeing much of a choice, I finally extended my hand.

"Deal."

Three

Before leaving the hotel, I returned to my room and collected a few things. I'd packed them just in case. I hadn't thought I'd really need the gun, but better safe than sorry. Since much of my work gear was safely locked in my car's trunk, and I wasn't expecting to be facing vampires, the single Colt 1911, nicknamed *Miss J* should be enough. Quietly, I turned the door knob and entered.

Like Barkley had said, Natalie lay fast asleep, beautiful and content, with only her left foot under the thin cotton sheet. I felt a wave of anger build, thinking about Anavash. Before leaving to meet Barkley, I'd covered the women with a sheet, but she'd gotten out of bed after I had left and didn't even have the courtesy to pull a sheet up over Natalie. Not only that, but no *Do Not Disturb* sign was on the knob.

My hands shook, and I felt a wave of heat flashing over my face. My frustrations hit the boiling point. Without thinking, I slammed my fist into the wall beside the door. It didn't do anything to help the situation, but I felt a little better.

Walking over, I sat beside my love and regretted every decision that'd led to this happening. If I hadn't been tired the day before, we could have driven for a few more hours and never stopped in this God-forsaken town. If my thirst for booze wasn't so strong, I would have been sober enough to see what Barkley and his minion were doing. Thinking of all the would haves and could haves weren't doing me a damn bit of good.

"This is my fault. It's always my fault. I keep finding ways of putting you in harm's way." I leaned over and kissed her on the forehead. Sitting back, I looked at her face and thought of the night before, when she graced the stage, singing her heart out with a demon at her side.

"One way or another, I'm going to fix this. I promise."

I pulled the covers up to her shoulders and shut the curtains. Stepping to the door, I put the *Do Not Disturb* sign on the knob, so she wouldn't be bothered or worse, found by the cleaning lady, who would most likely panic at not being able to wake her.

As I grabbed my stuff, I couldn't help but constantly glance over at her, sleeping so peacefully. I wondered if she could hear me. Was it a spell that had her sleeping so soundly? Something in the back of my mind kept telling me it was.

I crossed the room in haste. Grabbing the phone, I had the operator place a long-distance call to Nashville. Luckily, Miss Ellison, my neighbor and one of Nashville's benevolent witches, never ventured out of her apartment in the morning hours. When her sleepy voice answered, I didn't waste time.

"Miss Ellison, Thomas Dietrich. Natalie and I are in Memphis and have run into trouble. I need to know if there is a spell or some form of magic that induces sleep in its victim." The words came out rushed, but she understood.

"Let me think. Umm, well. There are any number of potions that can help a person sleep. There are a few spells that do the same," she said.

"The person who did this said Natalie will be asleep all day, maybe till midnight."

She was silent for a bit, and I almost thought we'd lost connection.

"Someone did this to Natalie? Oh, heavens, the poor thing. It sounds like the Sleeping Beauty spell.

Old magic, very old and very powerful. Whatever you do Thomas, don't try to force her to wake up. It can shock the system and cause who knows what kinds of problems. Best to let her sleep it off."

I heard rustling over the phone and then a tap, as if she put the phone down. I waited impatiently.

Finally, she returned to the call. "Thomas, I looked it up. A Sleeping Beauty spell usually lasts between six hours and twenty-four hours. The longest recorded duration was two full days."

I sat on the bed and lightly ran my fingers through her hair. "Two days. And there is no way to safely remove the spell or wake her up?"

"Sorry, Thomas, no. Best to leave her be until the spell passes."

"Thanks. I'll take care of things here," I said, hearing my voice shake.

I hung up the phone and continued gathering my equipment and thoughts.

I turned to leave but hesitated. It didn't feel right to leave her, alone and undefended. I'd find the penny, save her, and then someone would pay dearly. Demons maybe immortal, but while on Earth they can be made to feel pain. My hand instinctively moved to caress the handle of my pistol.

"Don't worry, sweetness. I'll be back later, and I'll make sure you're okay. I'll win your freedom, somehow. I don't know if you can hear me, but—I love you."

Stepping onto the sidewalk in front of the hotel a short time later, I took a deep breath of morning air. I felt weak, and my stomach growled. My mother always said a full day's work doesn't start off with an empty stomach. Checking my watch, I decided on a quick breakfast. A greasy-looking diner, situated a block away from the hotel, fit the bill.

The eggs tasted good, and the strips of bacon were just burnt on the edges, the way I liked, but everything seemed a little bland. I may have been sitting in the establishment, but I felt elsewhere. Without thinking, I kept holding my fork as if I were using it in a fight. My gaze moved from one person to another, looking for any unnatural signs. I'd been tricked and fooled by demons the night before, and now I knew I was overcompensating. Paranoia tugged at my fears. I needed to relax so that I'd be able to think straight.

As I sipped the third cup of strong, bitter coffee, my mind drifted, miles away, and I mulled over all the negatives of my situation. I tried to stay hopeful, but with only one thin lead, this would be tough. On the positive side of things, Barkley had given me some additional information. The strip club was also the state's biggest casino. Illegal, of course, but when did things like the law matter in these parts?

The penny, however, was a run-of-the-mill penny. Nothing about it was unique. But an idea came to me. If it were lucky, then you should be able to think of a side, heads or tails, and flip it repeatedly. If you have its luck, it should land on the side you pick, every time. It was only a theory, but worth trying.

I needed more information on the Golden Rhino, but asking random people on the street about a gentleman's establishment might not be the best course of action. My belly felt full, but my head still ached from all the drinking the night before. Barkley's elixir may have lessened it considerably but didn't cure it completely. The light pounding kept me from thinking at my best.

Glancing around, I observed the sidewalks filling up as workers began arriving in the city for the daily grind. Some drove their cars in to town, while others stepped out of the never-ending stream of buses, everyone on their way to the daily grind. I just couldn't understand how anyone could work that kind of a routine. Go to work, go home to a wife and kids, repeat daily until you die. That wasn't the kind of life I thought I could ever stand. When I was a kid, my mother said I was a born hunter. Solving problems, dealing with monsters, and hunting down the bad guys, it's what I do. And with Natalie in the picture, my life had become something worth living. Not that before her, I was suicidal, but I just didn't give a damn about myself, my life, or anything.

That daily grind, though, I knew she didn't want that kind of life. Me leaving for work each morning and coming home after a hard day's work, her having dinner on the table, and kids playing around. She wanted more. She wanted a singing career and for some reason, to also work with me in this crazy profession.

I laughed at myself and my thoughts of what she might want. Natalie lived life according to her own terms, which was one of the things I loved about her. No. The suburban routine would never suit her, or me for that matter.

My thoughts raced back to the image of her in bed, asleep until I succeed or fail. My chest froze at the thought of failing her, of losing her. I'd find a way to make this work. I'd find the damned penny, no matter what.

Something odd came to mind. All these men in suits, business suits.

Are they all from Memphis? How many are from out of town, here on business? What would a traveling business man do, after the work day has ended and he's in a strange town?

I snapped my fingers as I knew who to ask about the dark side of Memphis.

The desk clerk at the hotel.

My hotel stood nearby, and I took a look at the shimmering tower of glass, steel, and brick as I trotted towards it. My gaze moved from the top of the building to the main entrance. I felt a smile breaking through the pissed-off expression I'd worn all morning. The change in my expression actually hurt a little. I hadn't realized my face had been contorted in anger for so long.

In a jiffy, I felt my feet step from the hard concrete to soft red and gold patterned carpet of the Hotel Tennessee's lobby. The scent of stale cigarette smoke increased as I moved deeper into the lobby. The desk clerk smiled as I approached. His cologne did little to improve the smell. Instead it only assaulted the senses even more.

"May I help you? Mr. Dietrich, isn't it?"

I put on my best smile.

"I need some information. New to town and trying to get a feel for the place," I asked in a hushed tone. "A friend was out here a few weeks back and told me about a place. Ever hear of the Golden Rhino?"

His smile widened. "Yes, sir. Biggest, swankiest

strip joint in town." He waved in a practiced manner to my left. "When you step out the main doors, turn right and walk four blocks. It's on the opposite side of the street. But umm…"

The last part made me lean forward, concerned. "Yes?"

His apologetic voice was almost a whisper. "Well, the thing about the Rhino is… well, you see, they cater to a very select type of clientele."

"Rich?"

He nodded. "Wealthy, powerful, and important. They have a vetting system in place but given that you have the means to stay in one of our penthouse suites, I'm sure you'd have no problem getting inside."

"What has them so picky?" I found myself glancing to the open door of the hotel's bar, wondering if the sly demon still sat inside.

"The joint is billed as a gentleman's club, filled with dancers, card tables, and drink. But they cater to a lot of other tastes. You can get far more than just a dance from the ladies and gents. Hell, you can get whatever you want."

My eyes opened in surprise. "The police let them stay open?"

He laughed. "The police, the city government, even most of the big churches are all on their payroll.

Looking the other way in exchange for cash or romps with the boys and girls. And let's not forget about the casino. They've got one of the best set-ups in the Southeast."

"So how does a man get into a place like this?"

"Like I said, you have to be a man with power and connections. Miss Eva heads up the show, keeps the dancers in line and jiggling for all your cash. She's also notorious for match-making. You know, matches the best girls up with the richest clients, getting them addicted to a girl's kitty so they'll keep coming back for seconds and thirds."

He glanced from side to side. "It's no secret that a man with a big enough checkbook can just strut in there and buy himself one of the girls, as a wife or a kept woman."

I nodded. Every decent-sized city has at least one club like it. The practice was as old as the pharaohs.

"What connections do I need to get inside? I'd love to get in some card playing while my companion gets some much-needed sleep," I asked.

He tilted his head and gave me a sly look. Pulling out a small pad and pen, he jotted down some information.

"There is a gentleman that can help you at a nearby jewelry store. He is on Miss Eva's payroll and weeds out the… undesirables for her. To get inside, you'll need to prove you have the money to live up to their standards."

I nodded. "I guess you deal with some of the clientele. More than a couple of regulars?"

"The Rhino is an open secret in this town. A lot of their clientele stay in the hotel or work around here. As our manager likes to say, 'the richer they be, the more kitty they need.'"

He passed me the note but kept his hand over it as he looked me over. "Mr. Dietrich, they are picky, but you shouldn't have a problem getting inside. Good luck at the tables."

Four

As I walked away, I glanced down and read the note.

Brodnax Jewelers. Brodnax Bulding. Watch counter. Talk to Bobby.

"That shouldn't be too hard to find," I muttered to no one in particular.

My voice, albeit muted, seemed drowned by the noise of the city. I didn't as much hear my voice as knew I'd spoken. Falling into the flow of people on the sidewalk, I started on the next leg of my search for the mysterious Margo. Looking around, I couldn't help but feel bad for all these people. Everyone wore black or gray, making the city feel drab and dull. Not that I was one to talk, since according to Natalie, my wardrobe looked as dull as watching paint dry. Still, I felt strangely good in my new blue suit.

Most men ignored me, but the eyes of some of the women passing me glanced my way. Their approving nods seemed odd and gave me an uneasy feeling. In my line of work, I preferred not being noticed. Besides, I only wanted one set of feminine eyes on me, but at the moment, those were closed due to a sleep spell.

Feeling like I'd walked too far, I stopped and looked around. Where the hell was this damn place? I turned and started walking again, uncertain if this was the right direction.

One blond in a green dress, caught my eye. Diamonds sparkled in the sunlight. A lovely brooch and matching ear rings adorned her, giving me an idea. Several feet ahead and quickly moving towards me, I wasn't sure if she could really help but I seized on the opportunity. Given her accessories, I guessed this lovely lady may know the whereabouts of the local jewelry shops. I sidestepped to avoid running into someone and appeared right in front of her, almost running directly into the woman. She too had sidestepped in my direction for the same reason. We both stopped and laughed at the near collision.

The scent of Tabu Forbidden filled my nostrils. I loved the perfume's scent, musky with hints of sandalwood and plum. It'd become popular with a sect of witches in Nashville. A month earlier, I'd mentioned to Miss Ellison I planned on buying a bottle for Natalie. Without hesitation, she'd nixed the gift idea. Apparently, the makers were thought to have mixed it with elements of a dark love potion. That would explain its effects on men, especially yours truly.

"Oops, didn't mean to almost run you over. Say, those are some lovely stones you're wearing. Pardon me for asking, ma'am, but I'm new to town, looking for a jeweler, and I think I'm rather turned around," I said.

She cocked an eyebrow in a playful manner and cleared her throat. "You said a jeweler? Looking for a ring for your girlfriend?"

"Clever. I see what you did there. Truth be told, yes. My girl is sleeping in this morning, and I'd like to surprise her with a little something at dinner this evening." I watched as she thought and saw my moment to strike. "One of the bellhops at the Hotel Tennessee said I should check out Bord... no, Brod..."

"Brodnax Jewelers. Yes! They'd be who you'd want to go to for a nice ring." She paused, then asked. "They have the best diamonds, or are you looking for some other stone?"

"Diamonds, for sure." I said and remembered

something Natalie had once said a line she'd seen in a magazine.

No woman is truly a woman until a man's given her a diamond. Call it a rite of passage.

The memory of her laughing after reading it to me brought a smile to my face.

"I think it's a load of hooey. No woman neeeeeeds a diamond," she'd said, and then smiled as she gave me a side glance. "Not that I'm saying it wouldn't be nice to get one."

I inwardly chuckled at the memory of how she'd read the words to me, wondering what marketing genius had coined the phrase and gotten so many women to buy it, hook, line, and sinker. Not my Natalie, though I couldn't agree with her more. She sure as hell didn't need a rock to make her a woman.

"Any idea where they are?" I asked, and mentally made of note of the directions as she rambled them out.

"A block down this way," she gestured with her thumb. "Then make a right and go another block. Can't miss it."

Something about her seemed oddly familiar. Had I seen her before?

"So, you're traveling?" she asked. I nodded, and she continued. "Staying at the Hotel Tennessee?" Again, I nodded, and she continued. "Pretty swanky joint."

"I prefer only the best for my girlfriend, especially when we travel. This whole trip was a surprise for her. She's always wanted to go to New Orleans, so this trip is her birthday present," I said, watching her twirl a long strand of blond hair around her finger.

Hotel Tennessee? Good guess or did she know something? Nothing about her appeared demonic or suspect. Maybe my paranoia level was cranked up a few notches higher than usual after the events of last night.

The smile that crossed her face looked genuine. She stuck out her hand. I took it and gave a gentle shake. There was something about her firm handshake that didn't sit right with me. I sensed danger.

"Just call me Thomas, Thomas Dietrich."

"Luna Lavender. Maybe I'll see you and your girlfriend at the hotel..." She paused and glanced down. "I work across the street from it and occasionally stop in for drink at their bar when I'm in the mood to give myself a treat."

"Maybe so then," I said, tipping my hat.

I watched as she walked away, glancing back over her shoulder a couple times before disappearing into the crowd. Only from behind did I notice the backpack. Thin and made from the same fabric as the dress, it was almost hidden in plain sight. My heart raced, not from attraction but from danger. Something seemed too familiar about her. Had she been in the bar, last night? Was she working for Barkley too?

You're just letting the current situation get to you, old man, I thought.

Old man. I shook my head at the words. Decades ago, my teenaged sister, Lily, had been transformed into a demon, and since then hadn't aged a day in appearance. While she remained young-looking, every year and mile showed on my weathered face. Well, maybe not really to that extreme, but somedays, it felt like it. She'd taken to calling me old man a few years back. And now, she had me calling myself that too.

Proceeding down the sidewalk, I made a turn at the corner and walked another block, before seeing the sign, plastered on the front of the corner building. The Brodnax Building appeared to be an old yet well kept-up structure, probably predating the turn of the century. The windows along each side of the doors, were filled with various displays, showcasing the jeweler's wares. Far more than just the standard jewelry, the store showcased the finest and most elaborate home décor, works of art, and other items from around the world.

Stepping inside, I felt the temperature drop a few degrees. Beads of sweat on my brow, unnoticed before, suddenly cooled, leaving chilled lines in their wake. I hadn't realized how quickly the sun had heated up the city. The interior of the place would look appetizing to the wealthier community but looked overdone to my working-stiff eyes.

Beautifully carved and engraved display cases and shelves filled the place, with lights inside or shining down from above to illuminate their contents. The staff were all well-groomed and dressed to the nines. This wasn't a place for just anyone to shop. Brodnax catered to the wealthy and elite, and strangely, I felt right at home today.

Looking around and taking stock of the layout, I wove a course through the establishment. The watch counter sat near the rear and, in short order, I stepped up to it and nodded to the tall, slender gentleman behind it. He looked at me as if I'd stepped in dog crap and tracked it all through the store. His gaze moved back to the pocket watch he held and polished, ignoring me.

"A friend suggested I see a man named Bobby about a watch," I said, making sure my voice didn't carry too far.

He narrowed his eyes and tilted his head back slightly, so that he literally was looking down his nose at me. When he spoke, his voice rang with a high nasally sound.

"Is that so?"

"Yes," I said, tugging at the collar of my shirt. "A friend at the Hotel Tennessee told me you could help with information. You're Bobby, right?"

"I am."

His lips curled up, and his face conveyed contempt for my very existence. I knew the look well, but usually slapped it off the faces of the men who gave it. This time, however I needed information, so I put up with it.

"You're new to the city. Looking for entrance into a special place, I presume?"

I nodded and leaned over the counter, a bit. "Yes. The Golden Rhino."

"Judging from your accent and the..." he looked down at my jacket and sneered. "Flamboyant, if not rudely out-of-date manner of your dress, I'd say you were from Nashville. I'd imagine you're an entertainer, one of those God-awful twangy guitar players or..." He looked at my expression and apparently saw my cheeks reddening with anger. "You indulge in the arts, maybe a writer."

I wasn't sure if he was serious or just testing me. Swallowing my need to punch this snooty bastard, I just feigned a smile and chuckled. "I am from

Nashville. I was on my way to New Orleans for a vacation when I found a need to stop in your fair city for the night."

I checked my watch, making sure the embedded rubies along the edge caught the light. The watch had been a gift from the city, a token of appreciation for my help in stopping a particularly nasty vampiric crime wave, a couple of years back.

"As you can no doubt tell, we cater to a certain type of clientele, one who is above the need to ask the price of our wares." I gave a nod, and he continued. "You're curious about the Rhino?"

"I'd like to meet a specific girl who works there. Her name is Margo," I said, and watched him roll his eyes.

"Infatuated with the young lovely? I'll assume a 'friend' recommend her to you." He laid down the watch and polishing cloth and turned the full fury of his arrogance onto me. "Typical of some lesser men. A pretty young thing tickles their pickle in a halfway decent manner and then he has to tell the world about it."

Nodding my head, I chuckled. "Something like that, yes. I've never seen her, but she has… something I need."

He gave a questioning look I didn't bother addressing. Sighing, he asked. "What exactly do you need from me?"

"Let's start with the basics. Where it is? What do I need to do to get in? Aside from Margo, I hear there is gambling," I said.

He said nothing but looked down and tapped on the glass. When I didn't respond, he cleared his throat and tapped a little louder. I got the hint and looked down at the assortment of watches. I knew I'd have to buy something to loosen his lips. Luckily, I had a wad of cash saved up for the trip.

"The gold one with the saddle leather band, let me see it please," I said with a smile.

He rolled his eyes and looked at my suit with a sneer. "Does sir plan on wearing his new purchase with..." He paused and took a breath for effect. "This current wardrobe choice?"

"What's wrong with this suit?" I asked. His comments about Natalie's choice in my clothing were becoming annoying.

"Nothing's wrong with it, if you like the pre-war stylings of bland, half-witted designers." He raised an eyebrow, as if challenging me to say something back.

Is he a salesman or a damn fashion critic?

Natalie had picked out the suit, so I would wear it. Besides, it's the most expensive suit I've ever bought. So, what if it was a little out of style. A suit is a suit.

"Yes. I'll be wearing it with this."

"No, sir. That watch won't do. The band, the face, and the gold frame will only enhance the human tragedy that is your suit. If I can make a recommendation," he said as a grin appeared.

I nodded and observed as he carefully opened the door on the backside of the case, stuck an arm in, and withdrew a different watch. I took it from him and looked it over. The price tag, dangling on a thin white string didn't stop my heart, but the triple digits did make me swallow harder than planned.

"I'll just try this…" I tried not to swallow too loudly when I saw the brand name on the face. "Try on this Rolex while you enlighten me." I rolled up my sleeve and removed the watch I came in with.

Bobby told me the basics, the same stuff the desk clerk had explained. Then, he cleared his throat and finally got to the good stuff.

"The club's shows start around 6pm each evening, except Sundays, of course. The Blue Laws, you know. But the doors open early for members at 1pm. Miss Eva has a special lounge in the back for some of the city's more elite to relax, indulge in games of chance, and have special afternoon entertainment from the ladies and gents."

"What if I only need to speak to one girl in particular? Margo. Is there a way I could get inside for that?" I asked and looked at the watch. It did look stylish, and the colors worked well with my jacket.

"The girls don't usually 'just talk' with anyone that Miss Eva hasn't previously vetted. And even then, she'll want to know the topic of that conversation. Miss Eva is... especially particular when it comes to the behavior and doings of the ladies and gentlemen under her care."

"Sounds like she's one hell of a control freak," I said, and then gave an apologetic nod. "Sorry, that was rude of me."

"Perfectly understandable. Or more to the point, perfectly accurate," he replied. "The girls who work for her are housed in a hotel across the street from the club. The bouncers walk them to and from the hotel to the club, daily. Everyone going into the hotel is checked to ensure that no girl or guy is making a little extra on the side by hooking without permission. And of course, Miss Eva's specialty is providing a regular girl for men. I personally know the Mayor himself has routine visits with a young woman named Mattie, two, maybe three times a week." He saw my eyebrows rise and smiled. "It's an open secret about the Mayor and his adventures at the Rhino."

I cocked an eyebrow. "Miss Eva must have some serious control over the city if her customers are all of that caliber. Men in powerful positions, all over the city."

"And in the private sector," Bobby added and pulled a gift box from a drawer under the counter. "That makes her especially dangerous. So I do hope you'll understand that asking the wrong questions could lead a man, especially an out-of-towner, to an early demise."

I pulled off the watch and handed it back. My heart sank a little as he placed it in the gift box and gently closed it, smiling in the process. The more money I spent here, meant the less I had to splurge on Natalie, once I'd freed her, that is.

"I can provide you with a token to get into the club." He narrowed his eyes and pursed his lips as he continued. "But I can't guarantee that your Margo will be there this afternoon, or evening."

"Are you the club's personal gatekeeper?"

He chuckled. "In a way. Miss Eva employees a few people in positions like mine, positions dealing with the rich and powerful. I let them know about the club and the rewards of membership. And just as I work for her, I employee several people under me, who know which men to send to me for admittance. It helps avoid having the undesirables show up at the club's doorstep, only to be publicly turned away. Miss Eva prefers to avoid the kinds of unattractive displays that some drunk or boorish men can put on when they think they are being excluded."

Nodding, I pulled out my wallet. "So, Margo may or may not be there this afternoon. Is it possible for someone to get into the hotel where the girls stay?"

He turned and drew a small bag from behind the counter. As he lowered the box into it, he looked at me and shook his head.

"I wouldn't recommend it. There is a doorman at the hotel, someone with a boxer's physique, so I've been told. His duty is to allow only certain people."

Moving gingerly, he placed the bag on the counter in front of me and nodded towards the wallet. "With the correct type of token, you can get inside the hotel. But I can't help you with which room is hers."

I counted out enough bills to cover the purchase. Information in this town was a costly affair. "What type of token would I need?"

He took the greenbacks and pulled a black coin from his jacket pocket. "Present this at the club's door. It'll get you inside. This one is black, meaning that you're either new to the club or you've not paid enough to warrant inclusion in one of the higher echelons within its hierarchy. Paid members, depending on their standing with Miss Eva, may have red, silver, or even gold. Someone with a gold token would have access everywhere..." He cleared his throat, and a sour expression appeared on his face. "As well as access to any woman or man within the club's employ."

"You make them sound like slaves," I scoffed, but his serious expression gave me cause for concern.

"This is the south. Slavery never really went away. Folks like Miss Eva simply changed the way it looks. Who needs chains when a legal contract for a year's worth of services will suffice?"

I mulled that idea over for a moment. Lifting a coin off someone should be a piece of cake. An idea began to form, and I couldn't keep a smile from appearing. Flipping the token and catching it in my palm, I gave it a quick look over. It was about the size of a poker chip, metallic with a thin coat of enamel. Embossed on one side was the image of a nude woman, as seen from the front, hands on her hips and thrusting her chest out. Flipping it over, the same woman only viewed from the back appeared.

"Classy," I sarcastically remarked.

Bobby gave a curt laugh, then added in a flat, dry tone. "Yes, isn't it just?"

Five

Returning to the fresh air and sunshine, I strolled along Monroe Avenue, then turned the corner at South Second Street and saw what all the fuss was about. Honestly, I felt a little betrayed by all the talk about the grandeur of the Golden Rhino. Instead of a sultry palace of sin and debauchery, it appeared more like a drab and disheveled brick cube better suited to tax accountants than scantily clad dancers. Even the front doorway, sitting along the heavily used thoroughfare, looked as underwhelming as a plate of gravy without any biscuits.

Inwardly, I chuckled, but then it occurred to me. Why would they advertise? Given the sins conducted behind those walls, the Bible-thumping gentlemen who no doubt made up most of the Rhino's membership wouldn't want their activities to be common knowledge. I shook my head at that idea and inwardly smiled. It always seemed that most men who rally against drinking, gambling, and whoring were always the ones who secretly indulged in those vices the most.

Leaning against the corner of a nearby building, I pulled the gift box from my bag and freed the new and ungodly expensive watch. Rolling it in my hand, I glanced at the watch, but my primary focus was on the Rhino's main door. No one stood outside, but passing cars reflected enough light back through the glass doors to briefly illuminate a pair of well-dressed and well-armed men standing just inside.

"Tommy guns? A bit bold, don't ya think?" I muttered to no one but myself.

Slipping the Rolex on my wrist, I had to admit it looked great. Its gold face with an oyster style two-tone band worked well with the jacket, and with an easy maneuver, I snapped it into place. The hands were already set to the exact time, so I'd been told before leaving the jewelers.

The old watch felt heavy as it dropped into my inside jacket pocket. It may not be pretty but had sentimental value.

Something felt off with the world as I admired my new time piece again, as if my presence was known and I was locked in someone's gaze. Glancing back to the Rhino, I scanned the doors and then ran a quick look over the windows but saw nothing of alarm.

I noticed a man sitting on a stool across the street. His back was to me, so I knew he hadn't seen me. When he did turn back to look in my direction, it was quick. He was watching out for something.

Standing four stories, the hotel he guarded looked as dreary on the outside as the Rhino, but something told me it'd be a far different story inside.

I played a few scenarios in my head, but only one seemed likely to work. Go inside the Rhino, mingle with the locals and the girls, find Margo, pay for some private time, and learn about the penny's whereabouts. And if the Margo wasn't there? Then I'd find a man with a gold token, lift it off of him, and get into the hotel. It wasn't a good plan and had a million things that could go wrong. At the moment, however, I was stumped for a better one, so I'd see if I could make this work. For Natalie's sake, I'd make it work.

The best laid plans o' mice an' men, or so they say.

Not being a terribly religious man, praying didn't come naturally. This time, I whispered a silent plea to the big guy for help, reminding him that my success meant Natalie's soul would be safe. One less for the

Devil and all that.

I decided to wait and watch. Thing is, I didn't want to be conspicuous while I was at it. Just leaning against a wall and watching would eventually draw the wrong kind of attention. Then the sound of music caught my ears. Glancing across the street, I found the source.

A black man leaned against the corner of another building, gently strumming on a six-string and softly singing a tune I didn't recognize. The man looked like a heavyweight boxer instead of a struggling musician with a hat laid out, looking for donations. His crisp white shirt and black pants, along with a clean-shaven face told me he wasn't the type who lived on the streets or in slums like many street musicians I'd seen.

A handful of folks stood around him, listening, and dropping bills and coins into the overturned fedora at his feet. I couldn't have asked for a better cover. Stepping over, I blended into his following and let the music set my toes to tapping, but one eye stayed on the club's entrance.

Three upbeat songs passed the time before providence arrived in the form of an early 1930's Cadillac V16 Fleetwood limo. My heart skipped a beat as I admired its classic art deco inspired body, the pristine white wall tires, and an ungodly amount of polished chrome. The car slowed and then stopped in front of the Rhino's main doors. A man riding in something as stunning as this surely had a gold token.

Almost leaping from my stance, I crossed the lanes, easily dodging the oncoming traffic in the process, as the car's driver exited from the limo and casually walked around to open the rear door for his employer.

The elderly man who stepped from the Caddy reeked of unadulterated wealth and privilege. His blue eyes met mine as I strolled towards the club's door, and I swear, I could feel his mental judgement in the way he looked over my wardrobe choices.

What the hell was it with Memphis men and their dislike of my suit?

"Lovely afternoon isn't it?" I asked when he saw I was looking at him.

He narrowed his eyes, as if I'd crossed some unspoken line by not addressing him as *Your Highness* or something. His wrinkled left hand twitched towards my jacket.

"Can't say that I've seen someone wear something like that out in public in a few years." Although his words came out clear and concise, his soft-spoken southern accent was on full display.

"Hand-made by Gifford's in Green Hills. I like to dress to kill when out and about." I pulled on the lapels and smiled, making sure each word sounded steeped in an exaggerated southern accent. "I guess most southern gentlemen prefer the ordinary drab colors, but in the Music City, we like to do things with a little more pizzazz. Black and gray are fine, don't get me wrong. I just like making a statement. The boys playing the Opry taught me that."

Playing a part was routine in my line of work, especially the part of a country music mogul. That didn't mean I enjoyed it.

We reached the door just as the doorman swung it open, tipped his hat, and offered a welcome to us. I waved to the rich man to enter first. He nodded and smiled, as if I'd have dared go before him. As we stepped into the lobby, he glanced back over his shoulder.

"Dressed to kill? I hope you don't mean that literally." He laughed and proceeded to walk up to a large check-in desk, manned by a pretty brunette in a sleek red dress.

Sighing, I muttered under my breath, "We'll see."

The interior of the place was the exact opposite of the exterior. Rich wood paneling and trim covered the walls. Highly polished brass light fixtures hung everywhere, giving the otherwise dark room a soft, inviting glow. Large paintings of scantily clad women hung here and there, supposedly to tantalize the eyes of the beholders.

I knew they wanted to appeal to a certain clientele, but Jesus. Everywhere I looked, images of women in watercolors and oils, looked back and bared most, if not all of themselves in the process. It wasn't as much of an assault on the senses as it was an attempt at pushing the patrons to a point of sexual overkill.

"Jesus, people. Tone it down a notch or two. We already know it's a cathouse," I whispered.

To the side of the check-in desk stood a large pair of doors. Mr. Rich flashed his token, a gold one just like I thought he'd have. The young woman spoke a greeting and waved him to the doors. He glanced back at me and winked as he dropped the coin into his jacket's interior pocket.

"See you inside, Mr. Nashville." The old man laughed and disappeared through the doors.

Following his lead, I stepped up to the desk. Unlike Mr. Rich, who studied her plunging neckline and ample cleavage during his check in, I looked straight into her dark eyes. She smiled and gave an odd twist to and fro, as if inviting me to ogle.

"You're new to the Golden Rhino?" Her voice purred, and she tilted her head and bit her lower lip.

"Yes, ma'am. Just got into town. An old friend suggested I drop in and have a visit with Margo." I watched, but she didn't react to the name. "Is she working today?"

I held up my token and watched her eyes immediately focus on it.

The brunette cocked an eyebrow, and her lips curled upwards. "Black. Excellent. She should be in later for the show. It starts at 7pm. Margo and the all the other girls will be in the main lounge." She opened a binder and turned a few pages to today's date. I watched as her finger ran down the page. Name after name passed under her painted nail until she stopped at Margo's line. Off to the side was written *Not Available*.

Pursing her lips, she shook her head. "Sorry, sir, it looks like she is not in the club this evening."

Inwardly, I cringed because that meant having to get into the hotel to find her. But I played my part as the out of towner and kept a smile on my face. A table sat against the back wall, behind her. Flipping the token, I pretended to try and catch it, but purposely flicked it off to her side. My aim proved true as it hit the floor and rolled until it hit the back wall.

"Damnit. I've been nothing but clumsy today," I said, putting on a show of self-frustration.

She laughed as she spoke. "Not a problem."

The brunette stooped to retrieve it but ended up

having to crawl partway under the table. With her focus away from me, I reached over and lifted the pages in the binder. Flipping them, one at time, I let my gaze focus on Margo's line. Times appeared on most, but the last three days, *Not Available* appeared on each.

I dropped the pages and thought about it as the brunette backed out from under the table.

Margo, what have you been up to for the past few days? Disappearing from work or are you working for a special client? And gone when I'm supposed to find you and that penny.

She handed the token to me. "Here you are sir."

"No Margo? Well, my buddy recommended her specifically, but told me all the girls here at the Rhino are worth the trip," I said and put on my best smile.

"If you just go through the doors, they will lead to the main lounge. From there, you can go to the very back, down the hall, and try your luck at any of the tables. At this time of the day, the poker and blackjack tables should have some empty seats, but they will fill up fast." With a swift and graceful move, she placed her hand on mine. "And if you are eager for some company, just talk to any of the ladies inside."

Nodding, I faked a smile, which quickly faded as I walked away from her.

Walking into the lounge, the opulence stunned me. A well-stocked bar, made of mirrors and black marble ran the length of the back wall, with a huge stage, lined with burgundy velvet curtains, on the opposite end of the room. In between, stood dozens of tables and booths, all neatly arranged to get as many people as possible into the place. The joint looked like it could easily host a couple hundred patrons.

Only a dozen or so well-dressed men sat in here now, attended by half that many women. The waitresses wore almost scandalously short black dresses, designed to show a thin sliver of their bare backside. Just enough showed to draw the old men's attention and get them to want more. As I stood and observed, two old men slipped their hands round the ladies attending them and felt them up.

"Jesus, just get a damn room instead of making us all watch," I muttered under my breath.

After that display, I chose to ignore the tables and the women and stepped up to the bar. The music caught my attention, and I nodded my approval to the band's performance. On the stage, a five-piece jazz band played a seductive number with a wicked sax and a mellow tempo that matched my heart-beat. More than one of the women, walking from table to table, stepped in time with the drummer's brush slapping the cymbals.

Over the years, I'd faced down gangsters, monsters, and vampires, but rarely in a place like this. It looked far bigger than Voodoo Rumors, but it didn't seem to be a haven for vampires. Dangerous for sure, in its own ways, but not a home for the undead. At least, I hoped. Of course, the sun still hung in the sky and that meant sleepy time for vamps, no matter how big and bad they may be.

Waving the bartender over, I ordered a bourbon, neat. Giving me a wink, the young man put down his cigarette, which smoldered in a nearby ashtray as he prepared my drink. The scent of the Lucky Strips reminding me of how long it'd been since I'd smoked one. I resisted the urge to light up just yet. That didn't, however, stop me from inhaling deeply several times, sucking in that delicious albeit muted vaporized nicotine.

Drumming my fingers on the bar in time to the music, I waited until he placed on the glass on the counter before I started talking, putting on my best innocent traveler face.

"Just in from Nashville. A buddy of mine suggested this place."

He looked at me and nodded. The day was just starting for him. His cheerful expression and sparkling eyes told me what I hoped for: the man had plenty of energy and no customers, so he had time to talk.

"That so? Well, my friend, you've stumbled into the biggest pit of sin in the Southeast. You name your vice, and we cater to it. Drinks, cigars, cards, and all manner of playmates."

The latter vice garnered a wink and a grin from the young man.

"Miss Eva recruits only the finest ladies and top men from around the world to work in her establishment. Big, small, young and exotic. Have some from the Orient and a couple of French girls. And if you're into those twisted sort of encounters, we got us a real-life Nazi Dominatrix. They say she attended to Hitler, himself. She's sexy as hell but leaves bruises."

My eyebrow rose, and he grinned.

"I know what you're thinking. But hand to God, some of the richer boys here love having her whip them up one side and down the other."

"Any vampires?" I asked with a wink.

He laughed. "Not here. The Rhino is strictly human only. Maybe the only vice we don't offer."

I leaned closer and looked him in the eye. "My bud suggested a girl named Margo. I asked at the front counter, but the sexpot working it said Margo hasn't been in here in a couple of days. Maybe sick or something."

"I haven't seen her in a while, now that you mention it. Margo is one of my favorites. Has a heart as big as all outdoors. She's a great girl but not as attentive in the private rooms as she needs to be. Let's say that she's too picky, and in her line of business, you're expected to roll with whichever Joe or Jane is paying."

A middle-aged man approached the bar, waving and asking for Scotch.

"Hope you see her tonight," the bartender said, then stepped over to help the new customer.

Quickly draining my glass, I charted out what to do next. First, an accidental bump into Mr. Rich for lifting his gold token, followed by a trip to the hotel to snoop around and see if Margo was about.

I hovered at the bar for a while, and refilled and drained my glass again until I saw the old man rise from his table and head for the restrooms. I casually stood and fell in step behind him, mentally sizing the old man up and remembering which pocket the coin had gone back into after he'd shown it to the brunette at the front desk. Adjusting my tie, I smiled and flexed my fingers.

"Don't worry, I'm really not gonna kill you," I muttered to myself.

Six

Having spent several months in a state prison during my early teens, I'd learned a few things. The older thieves passed their time teaching the youngsters all the tricks of the trade. Skills, such as the proper way to rob a bank or where to shoot a man if you wanted to hurt but not kill, came in handy. But the most useful thing I learned during my time behind bars was the proper way to pickpocket.

The older thieves would put a rock in their pocket and the game was set. We younger ones would have to get the rock without being noticed doing so. If we got caught, we ponied up our dinner to them. If we succeeded, we got to eat.

Mr. Rich was too busy zipping up his fly to notice the well-timed collision until we slammed into one another.

"I am so sorry. All the excitement around here has me a little too distracted. If you know what I mean?" I laughed, straightened his jacket, and brushed off the collar.

His upbeat demeanor surprised me. "Perfectly understandable, my boy. Just ahhh..." His lips curled up, giving him a deviant expression. "Just don't get any ambitions about Ginger."

"Ginger?"

"A feisty redhead. She's my usual plaything. Eva and I have an understanding about her. Maybe you don't know how things work here, since you're new in town. Ginger is..." Still ginning, he slapped my arm and started towards the door, but stopped and turned. The happy expression suddenly faded to one of loss. "Well. She reminds me of my late wife, from back in the day when we were courting. Beautiful curly hair, and all those little freckles on her nose." He sighed and looked past me at something or someone, many years away.

Watching his expression soften, I suddenly felt bad for lifting the token. As lecherous as he may have been out front at the check-in desk, his reason for wanting a certain woman working the club made sense.

Remembering back to the night I met Natalie.

She'd come into Jerry's Bar, not to pick up a Joe for the night, but only wanted someone to talk with. Did Mr. Rich really want his red-head for sex or was he just reliving memories of a wife, dead and gone.

"Ginger. Feisty redhead. I'll mind my manners around her." I gave a slow nod and he responded with a smile.

A short time later, I flashed the golden token to the lone doorman at the Rhino's hotel across the street. Upon recognizing it, the large black man jumped to his feet, tipped his hat, and grabbed the door handle, smoothly swinging it open.

"Sorry for the delay, sir. You must be a new gold member. We've only gotta few, and I know them all." His voice came out deep but apologetic.

Touching the brim of my hat, I nodded. "Not a problem, my friend. Perhaps you can tell me which room Margo is in?"

"Second floor, room C," he said as I walked inside. I stopped and turned as he continued. "But she isn't in. She's indisposed."

"Sick or something?" I asked, trying not to sound too concerned. When he didn't answer right away, I added, "Look, my bud told me I should really hook up with her." I winked, which seemed to loosen the doorman's stiff demeanor. "Another girl will do, but

I've heard great things about Margo."

I reached in my pocket and pulled out a five-dollar bill. Folding it over, I slid it into his hand. "Surely you can help a man out? What's this girl's game?"

"Not sure I can help you too much. She's had the same gentleman caller, several nights in a row and then hasn't been sleeping here for the last three days. Not sure if the girl got bought or what."

"Sounds like some lucky man has found true love," I winked again and got a laugh. "Who would you recommend for a good time and a story or two about Margo?"

"Ginger. Second floor, room E," he said with a wide grin.

"Ginger? Red-head?" I asked, and he nodded in confirmation. "How many red-heads do they have here?"

After hitting the button, the elevator moved as slow as the post-man when you're expecting a check, so I took the stairs and found the door with a large brass E nailed to the frame. The strong smell of perfume, not one but a collection, filled the corridor. I swear, a different brand and scent hovered just outside each door, like a prelude of things to come for the woman behind it.

A gentle rap brought the lovely Ginger into view as she opened the door and greeted me. The smell of cigarette smoke and her expensive perfume assaulted my senses. Without meaning to, I tilted my head back slightly keeping my eyes on her face and trying to ignore the vision of her on full display in A translucent white nightie.

"My, my... what has Providence brought me today?" Her voice had a sweet southern charm that I immediately found myself fond of hearing.

Like her name suggested, she had that perfect ginger look: red hair, milky white skin, and a sprinkling of freckles that went all the way down.

"A man I met once mentioned that he could spend a happy lifetime playing connect the dots with all those little spots." I watched her smile grow. Mr. Rich hadn't said the words exactly like that, but it was close enough for me to break the ice with her.

She opened the door a little wider and nodded her head, encouraging me to enter. Ignoring her lustful beckoning, I gave a polite shake of my head. I had a deadline to meet. Two, come to think about it. Mr. Rich would eventually notice his gold token was missing and realize that our accidental collision in the restroom wasn't so accidental.

I thought about Natalie, while trying not to give the red-head the cold shoulder. Slipping a hand into my pocket, I palmed my money clip. I knew I could charm the information out of her in time, but I didn't have that luxury. Besides, I had a woman. Even in the line of duty, I didn't like flirting, especially now that feelings were growing between Natalie and me. As I peeled a pair of fives from the clip, glancing back and forth down the corridor. We were alone, so I looked her in the eyes.

"As much as I'd love to play, I'm kind of in a rush to help someone. One of your sisters in the biz, Margo, may be in serious trouble. I need answers to a few questions." I held out the cash, but she didn't move.

"You should talk to Miss Eva." Her eyes narrowed, and she slowly began to close the door.

Putting my foot in the way, I continued as I pushed my way into her room, slowly closing the door behind me. "One of Margo's regulars asked me to look into this matter. Miss Eva hasn't been helpful. Seems there's some contention between my client and your boss, and that places Margo in harm's way."

It was an assumption on my part, but something about it hit a nerve and made Ginger talk. "No. I guess she wouldn't want to help you or Margo unless it benefits her."

"Why is that?" I asked, and watched her hand lash out, snatching the cash from my fingers.

"If you know anything about our kinda business, then you know one of the conditions for employment is being willing to marry one of the club's regular sugar daddies. Miss Eva sets things up, the men pay out a lot of money for the girl, and a third of the cash is set aside for the girl to collect five years down the road."

I gave her a questioning look, and she added, "Miss Eva guarantees the girl will remain married for at least five years. Most stay longer, if not permanently since they're given new lives in Memphis' high society. Trophy wives, pampered and spoiled and given all the goodies a woman can imagine."

"I understand Margo has a regular man, who's seen her several nights in a row before disappearing?"

She shook her head. "Disappeared? No, no. Look, Margo wasn't the sharpest tool in the shed. The rumor mill's been saying Miss Eva is gonna give her the boot. Then all of a sudden, her luck changed, and she got this regular guy coming in every night for a month. She started breaking the cardinal rule and started seeing him outside of the Rhino this past week. She told me he was taking her out on the town a few nights ago, and I've not heard anything since."

"Think he bought her from Miss Eva?" I asked.

Miss Eva was nothing more than a modern-day

slave-trader, dealing in flesh for cash whether it was for a night, a year, or a lifetime. A far more sinister occupation than just being a madam at a brothel.

She smiled and rubbed her fingers together. Another five left my money clip and slipped between her fingers.

"You'd have to ask her. The man's name, however, was Bernard Bentington."

I thought about the name. It sounded familiar, but I couldn't put a finger on it.

Shaking her head, Ginger crossed her arms and smirked. "Bentington? You know, the railroad tycoon."

"Oh. Well, good for her. I guess good luck found her in spades." I chuckled, feeling a little sick at the thought.

Ginger frowned. "She said it was some good luck charm she got a hold of. Sure as hell need me one of those."

I waved another five. "Did she leave her stuff here? Sounds like she didn't pack up before that last date."

Snatching the cash, she nodded. "I have a spare key to her room. She and I share clothes and shoes a lot."

"Mind if I take a quick look around? She has something an important client lost. That's what all the fuss is about."

"Is there a reward?" Her expression conveyed concern, but then she licked her lips and narrowed her eyes as I gave a slow nod.

"A nice one, too."

I spent the next ten minutes going through Margo's apartment. The woman had plenty of clothes and jewelry, but no piggy bank. There were a couple of knick-knack boxes on a small bookshelf which contained several books of poetry and a worn-out copy of the Bible. But again, no penny.

I checked all the usual hiding places, under the mattress, behind the mirror and frames on the wall, but nothing turned up.

"Sorry you didn't find what you're after," Ginger said in a disappointed tone. "But come back anytime for another… look or something more."

Stepping back into the hallway, I tipped my hat. "Thank you kindly for your help."

Taking the same route out, I headed to the hotel's front door. The doorman jumped up and gracefully opened it. He nodded as I stepped through.

"That was quick." His quip brought a smile to my face.

"Yes, she was exceedingly delicious," I shot back,

generating a belly laugh from him.

"That she is sir. That she is."

Seven

Heavy traffic crawled between the hotel and the Golden Rhino. In both directions, cars inched along, belching out clouds of foul smelling exhaust. While I hated the smell, the traffic jam made crossing the street easier than it'd been just a short time ago. One driver, upset about having to slow from a crawl to a snail's pace as I walked in front of his Chevy, laid on his horn and yelled something out of his window.

I shook my head and laughed, thinking that no one ever blew their horn at me in Nashville. My good mood lasted all of about four seconds as my eyes locked on the doors to the city's palace of sin, reminding me of my deal and the consequences of failure.

I approached the check-in desk in the Rhino's

lobby. The beautiful brunette at the check-in counter had her attention on an elderly guest wearing gray, with a second man lined up behind him.

Pulling the gold token from my pocket, I positioned it between my thumb and index finger and waited. Once the man had checked-in, he walked to the main doors and struggled for a moment to open them. With the brunette's attention now focused on the next man in line, I acted.

Leaning forward a little, I swung my arm and released the token. It rolled, quickly eating the distance to the open door. I coughed loudly, drawing the attention of the older guest. He looked at me while the coin flew by his feet, rolling into the lounge. My memory of the club's layout proved correct, and a sizable amount of luck was in my favor. With only a few folks in the place, I saw the little gold disk rolling, unnoticed, deep into the room. It shot straight down the center aisle, coming to a stop a few feet from the table where its owner sat. I figured one of the waitresses would spot it and think it was carelessly dropped.

"Pardon me. Just adjusting to the climate," I said, faking another cough.

He narrowed his eyes. "This is Tennessee. It's pollen season. All the damn time, it's pollen season. The only time there isn't pollen in the air, there's snow on the ground instead." He shrugged and started to turn back to the door but hesitated. Instead, he gave a half-hearted point to the front door, behind me. "Not sure what's worse, damn pollen or that stink from the street."

At first, I thought he meant something crude about the rundown neighborhood, but the honking of a car horn corrected that assumption.

"I'd say the exhaust. Man wasn't meant to inhale smoke all the time." I said. The moment I saw his hand rise, as if he meant to protest, I added, "Except for a good stogie, that is."

The old man's face warmed as he smiled. "Good boy. Never underestimate the medicinal properties of well-rolled Cuban."

Turning, he walked into the club. Smiling at my luck, I took a spot in the line for the desk. When it was my turn, again, the brunette looked up and flashed her pearly whites. She leaned forward, doing her best to distract me with the ample amount of cleavage she displayed.

Everything about this place forced the idea of sex into the minds of its patrons. Fortunately, I had someone filling those needs. The only vice I worried about was the booze. It'd been a long, stressful day so far, and I'd only had the two drinks in the club earlier. Then, I remembered the ones I'd had in the bar with

Barkley.

"Back again so soon?" she purred.

"I'd like to arrange an audience with Miss Eva, please." Her expression darkened, and she hesitated, so I spoke again. "Nothing wrong or anything like that. But after experiencing her establishment, I'd love to talk to her about some business opportunities with my friends in Nashville."

I leaned on the counter and lowered my voice to a whisper. "Nothing illegal, mind you. But, certainly profitable. Ever been to Music City?"

The tone of her voice and the expression she wore morphed from sex kitten to corporate professional in a snap.

"Yes, sir. Been there many times. If you'd like to take a seat, I'll go inform her of your request and…" The flirtatious grin reappeared as she continued. "Let me see how many ducks she's got lined up to shoot, ahead of you."

The brunette closed the guest book, gave me another glance, then left through a doorway behind the counter.

I patted the holstered pistol under my jacket and waited.

Glancing at my watch, concern grew as to how long it'd be before Miss Eva sent a reception committee to escort me to her private office. Given her reputation, I wondered if lair might not be the better term for her office.

A colorful oil painting of a pair of nude women, kissing with their arms and legs entwined, hung over a padded bench. After a day of walking and running about the city, I needed to get off my feet for a bit.

"Ladies," I said to the painting, then took a seat beneath the lovers, captured in the oils, and waited.

Eight

A short time later, the hulking figure standing behind me in a three-piece suit, gave me a push, the kind usually reserved by demolition crews for knocking down brick walls. We'd reached the third floor, but he apparently didn't want to wait for the elevator doors to fully open.

"Inside." His voice had a mix of accents. Cuban and Jamaican seemed the most likely.

Stepping from the elevator, he passed me in the short hallway on our way to a door at the end. Some friends of his hovered behind me, waiting for me to make a wrong move. Their breathing reminded me of bulls at a rodeo, fired up in the bucking chutes and eager for a chance to throw the rider to ground and trample him to death.

I glanced to the man who'd opened the office door and now, waved me inside. Moments earlier when he and his goons came down to collect me, he'd introduced himself as Carlos. He firmly held my pistol in his left hand. With the amount of muscle on him, I had a sense it wouldn't take him much effort to crunch my favorite weapon into a chrome-plated ball of steel.

The other two men who'd escorted me to the office door were a tad smaller, yet still impressive. Miss Eva obviously liked her men large and formidable. While muscles are good to have, I've found the greater muscle is the one between a man's ears. Give me brains and sleight-of-hand over brawn any day.

And maybe, a vial of holy water, just to be sure.

Looking around as we entered, I ignored the woman in the room. I didn't want to give her the impression she could intimidate me since her smug expression and cross-legged position behind her desk seemed to imply that was what she was used too.

The office was larger than I expected. Bookshelves lined the left and right walls, while thick, blood red curtains hung on the far wall. Brass light fixtures hung on either side of the room and illuminated the large desk and the chair behind it, while small stained-glass lamps washed sections of the room with vivid colors.

Carlos stepped up, laying my pistol and my wallet, which had also been liberated from me downstairs, onto her desk.

"He had this on him, along with a black token."

Slowly, she opened my wallet and extracted my ID. "Mr. Dietrich? Interesting. You may call me Miss Eva. All of this around you is my domain. My own corner of the universe, if you will. Now, I understand you have a unique business opportunity for me?"

The woman behind the desk spoke with a thick, southern accent, but there was something off about it. The words lacked emotion, empty of any indication she gave a damn about me or anything else around her.

Tilting her head, she studied me, and a curious smile warmed her cold features. When she spoke again, a hint of playfulness came out in her tone.

"You look familiar. I don't think we've met in person, but I know that jaw line and those eyes. They've seen some nightmares, haven't they? Of course, I know the name."

Miss Eva slowly rose from her chair. The black and white number she wore enhanced her figure and was the perfect contrast against the long red locks, cascading over her left shoulder.

Jade, so perfect it almost glowed under the lights,

adorned her lobes and neck. Again, a perfect contrast to the dress and the hair. The pearly green almost matched her cold eyes.

"I get half a dozen shysters a week, coming in here, offering up the world for a chance to meet me." She walked around to the front of the desk and leaned against it as she looked me over.

Crap, I thought.

I'd been so preoccupied with getting into the office and how to handle the hulking figures escorting me here that I'd failed to plan out what to say if I got this far. My time in the lobby had been spent worrying about Natalie and how to explain all this when she woke up.

"Ummm, yes," I said, hoping I wasn't sweating too much.

Everything about my life in Nashville shot through my thoughts, collided, and merged, and then it hit me. The story would be a lie, a big, fat lie, but a believable one. I hoped.

"I'm Thomas Dietrich, just like my ID said."

She ran a playful finger across her chin as her lips curled upwards. "The face looked familiar. Now I know why. Our papers, like those in Nashville, always downplay or flat out lie about the monsters in our lands. But one of our city's rags has done a number of write-ups about your battles and righteous deeds in our state's capital. They've printed a few stories and photos. Let me see if I remember what I've read about you?"

She hesitated, and I could see the wheels turning in her mind.

"Nashville's notorious monster hunter, Private Investigator, war hero, brother of Nashville's demonic brothel-owning vampire, Mistress Lily, and, oh yes, the man who single-handedly stopped some kind of behemoth in the South Pacific. You're *that* Thomas Dietrich, right?"

Trying not to swallow too hard and give away my concern, I smiled and gave a nod. This woman knew far more about me than she should and that sent a cold shiver down my spine.

"Well, I don't like to brag, but you've done your homework."

She gave a nod. "I got a call from my people in the hotel that you checked in yesterday. I make it my business to know everyone of importance that stays in or passes through my city. It was you and a young woman. Not your sister though, right?"

"Correct," I said and watched her eyes open a little wider.

"Too bad. I'd like to meet your sister," she said, sounding genuinely disappointed. "Voodoo Rumors is my only real competition within the state when it comes to providing sex to hungry men and women. Although I didn't have to sell my soul to Satan in exchange for…"

She purred and gave me an unexpected look over. "A house full of bloodsucking girls. You know, bitten at just that right time in their youthful years. Their age frozen at that perfect moment when they have those sorority girl looks that men fork over their fortunes for. But only women. She doesn't cater to men who like the masculine form, does she?"

"No. Just womenfolk. The churches in the midstate are a little more influential than they are out here. Besides, Lily prefers women."

She scoffed. "So, I've heard."

Looking at the thick curtains, I asked, "So, no vampires here?"

Her brows rose. I think my question surprised her. "No. Tried it once, but the fangy things are too difficult to keep under control. I guess you have to be a monster to control a monster."

"True." I said, and cleared my throat, hoping to sound convincing. "My sister's establishment isn't quite the size of your joint, but we've got room to grow. Lily has all the right connections to the best and brightest in Nashville: politicians, musicians, and all the top cats with wads of cash they don't mind dropping on girls and the tables."

She nodded and gave a halfhearted smile. "And?"

"I'm thinking of an alliance of sorts. We've got all of Nashville's finest and wealthiest men in our club nightly. Most of the Governor's staff are regulars, so Lily has influence over the whole state. Now imagine if we cross-promote. We send our regular customers down Memphis-way for vacations along the mighty Mississippi River, and you send some of yours up our way."

I put on my best smile. "Couldn't hurt anything. Only give us a chance to tap into the vacation funds of our clients. Keep them from heading to Cuba, L.A., or New York to spend all that extra cash. Plus, we could set up a rotation of talent, you know, sending our singers, dancers, and ladies back and forth. Keep a constant flow of new blood, so to speak, coming in so we keep the clientele happy."

"Lily's girls are vampires. How would I keep them under control? As stated, I've not had that kind of luck." She crossed her arm and stared at me.

With a smile, I answered. "Not all of the ladies at Voodoo Rumors are vampires. Only about half. The rest are happy, bouncy humans, just well controlled by Lily." I saw her tilt her head to the side, questioning that. "Let's just say that it's a demonic thing she can do."

The idea sounded sensible, although I hated doing

anything that promoted Lily's den of sin. Still, I hoped that Miss Eva didn't know about my opposition to vampires and the club. She already knew too much about me. Only my relationship to Lily might make this work.

"Word is you routinely kill vampires." She toyed with a jade orb hanging from a gold chain around her neck as she tilted her head again and waited for my response.

"Well, yes. I do kill vampires... and werewolves, demons, and the like. But if you know about Nashville's monster subculture, you'll know Voodoo Rumors isn't the only den for the undead. Lily keeps her pets on a tight leash. It's the rogues I put down."

She said nothing, just stared.

"Lily is well connected with the Vampire Cartel. If you have an interest in including vampires on the list of fetishes you cater to, we can make it happen. Only the best women and men for a potential partner." I bit my tongue, thinking about how I'd shut the Cartel's vampire trafficking down for the foreseeable future a couple of months ago.

Her voice flattened, showing a lack of interest again. "Yes, I know about the Cartel and its trafficking hub in our state's capital."

Sighing, I shrugged my shoulders. "She's my sister, so I do what I can to help out the club, and she keeps her vampiric dancers off the streets. I keep her and her crew alive. It is not a perfect arrangement, but the best of a bad situation, and of course, I get a cut."

I noticed a sly grin forming as she spoke. "And what are you really wanting? I doubt you'd make this kind of offer unless you needed something to start things off."

"Want?" I asked.

"Hun, anytime a man walks into my club, offering up a deal like this, there's always something he wants up front." She approached me, filling my nostrils with the scent of honeysuckle.

I chuckled. "Well, now that you bring it up. There is something a friend of mine needs, something I think one of your girls may have acquired."

I watched as she cocked a perfectly shaped eyebrow at me.

"And what is that?" she asked, tilting her head.

When I didn't give a quick answer, she made a motion with her index finger. Carlos, who'd been hovering behind me, stepped up and grabbed my right arm. In an embarrassingly easy move, he had my arm twisted behind me.

His breath felt heavy on my neck as he spoke. "I think you owe the lady an answer, monster hunter."

I struggled, which only made Carlos push my arm up, sending bolts of lightning into my shoulder.

"Do you always interrogate men in your office? Seems like you'd have a special room," I said, not letting any emotion seep into my words.

Anger rose in me, but I'd be damned if I was going to let her think she was in charge or that her men were getting to me.

"Usually," she said, and twitched her fingers at me. "Just go ahead and answer. Carlos hasn't broken anyone's arm in a few days, and I know he's itching to do just that."

"A friend lost a valuable penny to your girl, Margo. Well, the coin has more of a sentimental value to him," I said as nonchalantly as I could, given the circumstances.

"This coin must be worth a pretty penny, if you'll pardon the pun. See, you're the second man to visit today, looking for Margo and this mysterious penny."

"Oh? And who else is looking?" I asked, not letting her see my surprise.

She hesitated and looked me over again. "A tall, imposing fellow named Mr. Barbas. He's offered me the world for its return."

Stepping close, Miss Eva repeated. "Offered. Me. The. World. For its return."

Clearing my throat, I took a more serious tone with her. "Mr. Barbas isn't the only one who wants the penny. The man I represent is willing to pay big bucks for its return."

Her brows rose in surprise, but it only lasted a couple of seconds.

"Mr. Barbas requested I kill anyone who comes here for the coin. But if there is money to be made or power to be claimed, perhaps I should keep it for myself? Margo did slip-up, you know. The silly thing told me the coin's secret power a few days back."

"So, you have it?"

Noticing her eyes dart to a picture on the wall, things fell into place. I wouldn't be able to take out all three of the oversized goons, but I knew where the coin was, and that was half the battle. I needed to escape from here and break back into the office at a later time.

"While your offer is tempting, Mr. Dietrich, I'm afraid I must decline," she said, and slowly walked back behind her desk.

"My boys are going to take you out back and rough you up a little. A shame to bruise up such a yummy-looking physique but be happy that's all I'm having done to you. Take some advice, Mr. Dietrich. Don't come back here. Oh, and tell your interested party that the penny is not for sale."

She paused as she lifted a cigarette from a box on the desk and placed it between her perfectly painted lips. In a quick but graceful move, she lit a match and then the cigarette, letting the first hints of smoke boil from her nostrils.

"But if your mystery client wants Margo, I'd suggest looking around Bentington Manor. Old Bernard swooped in and took a shine to the fair young thing, and just in time too. She was losing money for me, and I was about to let her go. Guess the luck of that penny really paid off for her. He bought her at a generous price, didn't even negotiate the deal, so I made a killing off her. Our dear little Margo has already started her new life as the latest trophy wife in Memphis' elite."

"And you kept the penny?" I asked, knowing that she felt in charge of our situation. I'd play her ego and let her tell me too much.

She nodded. "I made a deal with her. If I got the penny, she could get released from her contract and marry the tycoon. After all, she didn't really need its luck anymore. She's got a rich husband now who can buy her all the luck she'll ever need."

"Good for her," I said sarcastically.

"Boys, don't hurt him too much but make sure he gets the point." She looked straight at me as she added. "I'm only letting you live because I've had an interest in doing business with your sister. And like I said," She looked me over again and let out a sigh. "You're all kinds of delicious, for a man your age."

Carlos clamped down on my arm again, but as he swung me around, I tugged against the man's attempts to drag me from the room, partly in show and partly out of habit. As we reached the office door, I heard the elevator's bell ring as it reached this floor. All five of us looked around in surprise since no one had called for it.

Two suited men escorting a large black man stepped from the elevator. I immediately recognized him as the street musician I'd seen earlier. Growling, he bared his teeth and narrowed his eyes. This guy looked ready to unleash the fires of Hell on this place. Maybe it was a good thing I was being taken out back to be roughed up.

"Esteban, what's this?" Carlos asked, loosening his grip on my arm. I wasn't sure if it was intentional, but I chose not to take advantage of it. I'd wait to see if one of the other guys made a mistake.

"We caught him in the kitchen. He got past our boys out back," the goon holding on to the black man's right arm answered. His accent came out so thick, it was difficult to understand him. "One of the cooks said he saw Danny flying over the fence out back. You know, the ten footer. The rest of the boys guarding the place back there are gone."

Miss Eva cleared her throat. With a hard jerk, Carlos pulled me to the side, clearing a path between her and the imposing black man. The air, already thick with tension, took on an even darker feel, like every shadow suddenly weighed a thousand pounds.

Miss Eva sighed, showing her disappointment, and every man in her employ shifted into new positions, ready to launch themselves at the black man should he try something.

"Don't you know colored men aren't allowed in the Golden Rhino? Or maybe someone as dark as you can't read the signs on the door. Is that it, BooBoo? Monkey can't read the big words?"

Her voice purred as she slung each verbal jab at him. To his credit, he didn't react, only smiled in a way that made me concerned for my safety. She stepped closer to him, moving within reach of me, something Carlos seemed to notice, as his hand tightened again, holding me in place.

"That's a nice shirt for a gorilla. Looks like silk. Probably cost someone a fortune. I imagine you stole it."

He cleared his throat in a way that sounded like a laugh and in a polite tone began speaking. "No, ma'am. Not stolen. I'm a private detective from South Carolina. My name is Dexter Wolf, and I've been hired to find someone in your employ. One of your girls. Her name is Margo."

Miss Eva's laugh seemed to be an invitation for

her men to join her. Their amusement lifted some of the tension, but I suspected the resolution to all of this wouldn't be pretty for them.

Crossing her arms, she smirked. "Am I supposed to be impressed? Your client must not be a man of means or class. No one with any sense of standards is going to hire an uneducated black man who calls himself a detective."

She leaned closer to him and laughed. "Did you splurge and get cards printed up? Could you even spell detective, or did you just have them print 'Private Dick?'"

Now he smirked. "Dexter Wolf, Private Detective and Consultant. Oh, and I have a doctorate in psychology from Fisk University, in addition to my private dick license."

The room rang with laughter until he spoke again. This time, his words had a sharp edge. "Ma'am, I've had a long couple of days, and I'm on a bit of a timetable here. So, tell me where Margo is, and I may not bust up the place and your men."

Carlos let go of my arm and nodded to another man to take his place at my side. He drew a chrome-plated revolver from his jacket. "Was that a threat, blackie?"

Nine

Quickly assessing the room only served to confirm our dismal position. Outnumbered, certainly. Out gunned, absolutely. Out classed? From my viewpoint, that seemed debatable.

Wolf's size could easily be compared to an Olympic weightlifter. He had the muscle to make life hard for at least three of them, leaving me to deal with the other two. Assuming we could work together, and he knew I wasn't part of Miss Eva's entourage. Of course, being manhandled by Carlos in front of him, should clue him in on things.

The office might have been spacious, but in a fistfight with this many people, their numbers only made it harder for us to miss. Being on their own turf might make them over confident, something we could use to our advantage. Of course, they had the guns.

Wolf sighed as he looked at the pistol in Carlos's hand and then to Miss Eva. "Like I said, tell me where Margo is, and your boys will live to see tomorrow, assuming they behave themselves. Otherwise, a world of hurt is about to happen to them. And I won't be responsible for any of the property damage that occurs when I throw these boys through your walls."

Grunting with anger, Carlos marched straight towards him, murder in his eyes and his pistol outstretched. He didn't stop until the barrel was pressed into Wolf's forehead, pushing the man's head back.

"Ma'am, just say the word and this boy's brains will see some daylight," Carlos said, tensing up, prepared to shoot.

"Is it always this exciting around here? And I thought Nashville was a tough place to live," I joked. I forced a chuckle but no one else did.

Wolf looked at me, tilting his head. I saw the moment he realized I was on his side, as the man tried to suppress his smile.

I looked to Miss Eva and watched as her lip twitched. Before she could get the first word out, I yelled to Wolf, "Make your move!"

I didn't see his arm move, only saw it change

position, but now he held the shiny, chromed pistol. Carlos stepped back, looking at his shaking his hand, apparently shocked he'd been so easily and efficiently disarmed. Wolf held the gun in both hands, and with seemingly little effort, bent the barrel ninety degrees.

The man on Wolf's right, the one named Esteban, grabbed Wolf's arm and tried to jerk the black man backwards. The expressions on both their faces were priceless, one annoyed beyond belief and the other showing sheer terror. I suspect Esteban's attempt was the last conscious thing he did that day.

Wolf grabbed him and slung him around with super-human strength, sending most of him through the wall beside the door. Splintering wood and plaster dust filled the air as the wall seemed to explode from the impact. Only the man's feet could be seen, sticking out of the hole and not moving.

The man who still held my arm, predictably, let go and reached for his pistol. I threw myself at him, hunching forward and putting all my weight into the attack. My shoulder connected with the right side of his rib cage, bouncing him back into the bookshelves. His pistol, barely out of its holster, slipped from his fingers and dropped to the floor.

Before he could get his bearings, I slammed my right fist into his face, followed by three quick jabs from my left. A bit dazed, he stepped forward, twisting and swinging a left hook at me. I jerked myself back, letting his fist pass in front of me.

I shoved him back with all my might, then took a step and sent a kick into his groin. Air huffed from left his lungs as he doubled over. I charged him, grabbing his hair in my hands and slamming the back of his skull into the shelves. He dropped to my feet like a sack of potatoes.

Seeing movement to my left, I spun towards Miss Eva. She had her back to me but spun with my pistol in her hand. Without hesitation, I grabbed her right wrist, twisting it as I pulled it over her head. Defiantly, she attempted a kick to my shin but missed. I shoved her back, ripping my gun from her hand. She stumbled backwards falling back onto, her desk.

"Nobody points my own gun at me," I roared.

Turning, I saw the hallway had become a scene of devastation. The broken bodies of four well-dressed men lay sprawled about with Wolf standing over them, brushing plaster dust off his shirt and pants. He looked at me and then to the goon I'd put down.

"I could have taken him too," he said in a voice that matched the rolling sound of thunder.

Nodding, I motioned back to Miss Eva. "I know but I wanted to impress the lady."

With a panicked expression, Miss Eva scurried to

get behind her desk. Before she could move around the corner, I grabbed her by the arm. Her green eyes bore into me.

"Get your hands off me, you worm," she hissed.

"Be nice, and I will be in return. Now, where is Margo?" I asked, before leaning a little closer to her. "And more importantly, where is the penny?"

Her free hand flashed upwards, slapping me hard across the face. An immediate but short-lived burn irritated my skin, but I took the attack in stride. It hadn't been completely unexpected.

"Again, be nice or else. The penny?"

When she scoffed, I added, "Let me guess, some place predictable like your safe?"

Wolf stepped up and put a hand on the back of my neck. I could feel his fingers pushing my blood vessels closed as he spoke.

"Who are you and why are you after the penny?"

Pushing Miss Eva away, I grabbed at his hand. Turning my head as far as I could with his hand on my neck, I answered. "Thomas Dietrich. Trying to save my girlfriend."

I saw his eyes widen and then narrow as his lips twitched upwards at the corners. He nodded as his fingers loosened their grip.

"I'm not from around here but I know the name. Always pictured you as taller with more muscle." He let go just as my head started spinning.

"Yeah, I get that a lot," I responded.

"Sorry, but I need the penny. A young life is at stake," he said, and moved to my side, looking down at Miss Eva, who sat awkwardly on the edge of her desk.

"I think you'd better open the safe," I said to her, pulling her upright and clamping my hand around her arm.

Her response was broken and shaky as she squirmed. "One scream... and I'll have... a dozen more... men up here."

Miss Eva's eyes widened, and her gaze darted back and forth between us. Her teeth clenched and a primal groan, sounding like a wounded animal, bellowed out.

"Think we can't handle that?" Wolf said, turning to look me over. He shrugged. "Yeah, we can handle that. Eleven for me and one for him."

"Thanks," I muttered.

"Don't mention it," he replied.

Having only met the man two minutes ago, I had to admit I liked him.

Miss Eva sighed and slumped her shoulders, admitting defeat. Her body relaxed somewhat as some measure of confidence or composure seemed to reemerge in her demeanor. "I'm not going to open it for you, and this gorilla maybe strong but even he doesn't have the muscle to rip the door off."

"I'm willing to put that to the test," Wolf said, and smirked.

Her fear began evaporating like spilt moonshine on a sunny July afternoon. "You boys don't have a chance in…"

Her words trailed off as her eyes focused on something off to the side. Turning my head, I saw a framed painting, the one she'd glanced at earlier, swung out on hinges with a safe door behind it. At first, the logical assumption seemed that it'd gotten jarred open during the fight. But then the dial moved, and a chrome handle twisted slightly. With a subtle click, the metal door swung open.

"We're not alone," I whispered.

Items in the safe moved and without warning, two stacks of twenty-dollar bills lifted and flew out into the room, spraying bills out in all directions.

"Watch yourself. It's a distraction." I said, knowing that the movement of the bills as they wafted through the air could mask someone who didn't want to be seen.

Letting go of Miss Eva, I looked around as a familiar scent washed over me, pulling at my memories. Wolf stepped closer and took a hold of her a moment later.

"Tabu Forbidden," I whispered. "There is another woman in here."

"What?" Wolf asked. "What other woman?"

I stepped to the side. I'd seen too many strange things over the years to rule out the impossible. Turning and stepping lightly, I kept my eyes on the hallway. It was a hunch, but if this woman was invisible as I suspected, she might give herself away.

A well-performed spell, conjured by a talented witch, could easily render someone else or herself invisible. Miss Ellison had spent years tutoring me on the types of magic used in the world and how to spot a spell and its caster.

Sure enough, a foot-print appeared in the hallway in the fallen plaster dust. I launched myself at the mysterious intruder. I never saw her but felt the impact and heard her grunt.

She and I both fell, but I wrapped my arms around her as we dropped onto the mix of floorboards and broken bodies. The invisible woman struggled, but I held her in check and then just sat there.

"Just give it up, sweetheart. You're not going anywhere," I said.

She struggled a little more, kicking and tossing herself back and forth, but I kept my position. Then a thought struck me, and my mood darkened.

"Whatever coin you have, it isn't the right penny.

We've all been duped."

The woman whispered a series of broken words and appeared. I looked down into icy-blue eyes, framed by blonde locks. We'd met before, on the sidewalk.

"Well hello. Miss Luna Lavender, wasn't it? This isn't your luck day. Wrong penny."

I could see confusion in her expression.

"Mind climbing off of me and explaining what the hell you're talking about, handsome?" she said with an accent that I couldn't quite place. Not northern, but not southern. Then it hit me, the woman might be from the Midwest.

Standing, I held out a hand which the lady graciously accepted. Once on her feet, we both looked at one another over, sizing the other up. She wore a black jumpsuit with black boots and a black utility belt with several small leather pouches attached. The green backpack I'd seen earlier was still in place.

I held out my hand, palm up and cocked an eyebrow. Looking annoyed, she fished a penny from one of the pouches and placed it in my palm.

I motioned to her suit. "Nice outfit. A little different from the dress."

"The dress doesn't help me when I'm working. Too many things a skirt can get snagged on when skulking about," she replied.

"What makes you think it isn't the right penny?" Wolf asked from behind me.

Luna and I turned and approached him and Miss Eva. I flipped the copper coin a couple of times, noticing the side. Each time, I said, "heads," but only once did it come up as I wanted.

"Heads," I said, flipping it a third time.

"Tails," Wolf said, looking at the caught coin.

I repeated the action four more times, calling heads on each flip and getting tails in return.

"It brings good luck to whoever owns it. If Miss Eva had the real penny, we'd never have gotten this far. If our invisible friend with the sticky fingers had gotten the real thing, she'd never have been caught or spotted," I said, stepping closer to Miss Eva.

Annoyed, Miss Eva shook her head. "The little bitch gave me a fake one? I'm gonna kill her before this night is over with. I'll have a contract on her pretty little head as soon as you leave."

"All things considered, now that all the world's luck is on her side, do you really think anyone can kill her?" Wolf asked.

A deep gravelly voice echoed through the room. "She can be killed, but is that really how you want to retrieve the coin? Seems like cheating, in a way. Takes the sport out of the game."

I turned to see the white-suited demon, Barkley,

standing in the doorway, a cigarette in one hand and a tumbler of alcohol in the other. As always, he wore a smug grin as he stepped into the room, not caring to avoid walking on the fallen bodies of Miss Eva's men.

Pointing, he said, "You, woman—Eva, take a seat behind your desk." When she failed to move, he added, "Please."

We all looked at one another and then watched as she reluctantly moved and sat as instructed. Barkley walked to the desk and raised his hand holding the cigarette. Moving it in a circular motion, the burning tip of the cigarette began to glow a little brighter, leaving a burning streak hovering in the air.

"Watch, my dear. Relax and sleep," he said, and then turned to the rest of us as if nothing had just happened.

When I glanced back to Miss Eva, her head had tilted back, and her eyes had closed. For the first time since we'd met, she looked peaceful. The powerful owner of the Golden Rhino was gone from this world, at least for a while.

"What the hell is this, man?" Wolf barked, taking an oddly familiar tone with the demon.

"Yeah, you didn't say anything about others being after the penny," Luna chimed in.

Barkley took a long draw on his cigarette as he

looked around at the collection of misfits before him: a monster hunter, an apparent witch, and a black hulk.

"This is nothing you should fret over. I needed to make sure I'd get the penny by midnight tonight."

He pointed to me and then to Wolf. "I hadn't planned on the three of you meeting like this. Oh, I felt certain you'd cross paths in some manner, since you're all after the same thing. I mean really, gentlemen and lady. Why use one detective when two doubles the odds of the coin's return. And surely having an infamous thief like Luna Lavender on the hunt would only increase my odds."

"Infamous? Never heard of her," I said, and looked to Wolf. He shook his head as well.

She sighed, "I change my name as often as I change my panties. When you work on the wrong side of the law, you learn to keep a low profile. A new name and a new look for every city I visit."

Wolf cracked his knuckles and squared up to Barkley. "When you brought me to this city, you didn't list these folks as part of the deal. You make the same promise to them too? They playing your game for the same reasons?"

"What?" Luna exclaimed. "Wait a damn minute. We have a deal. I get your precious penny in exchange for you erasing my mother's testimony in the police records."

"Police records?" I asked.

Luna looked at the floor as she answered. "My mother did some stuff, years ago for the mob, then she became an informant. It doesn't matter right now."

Barkley walked to a small drinks table, sitting near the burgled safe, and poured a couple of finger's worth of bourbon into his glass. He studied the label for a moment and frowned before pouring another couple of finger's worth on top of what was already there.

"All the money in the world and she buys swill like this. I guess good taste doesn't always come to those with riches." Turning, he took a long sip of his drink, winced, smacked his lips at the taste, and looked the three of us over.

"You each have gifts and talents needed for a job like this. I'm certain one of you will succeed. Three of you triples my chances of getting the penny before Barbas does."

He hesitated and then took another sip of the swill. "Remember, this isn't about you. As far as I'm concerned, this is all about me getting the penny. So… make it happen."

He turned and walked into the hall. Without turning around, he held up the glass and added, "You have a long night ahead. Don't disappoint me."

Ten

Leaving the Golden Rhino turned out to be less of a problem than trying to get inside. Most of the security staff was in no condition to stop us or to even stand. A short distance from the place, Wolf mentioned a small diner a couple of blocks away, so we decided to make our way there.

"I'll trail behind to watch your backs in case any of those goons get brave," Luna said.

'How…" I started to ask, but remembering her little trick, I realized she had a good point and a better plan.

She muttered some broken words and darted to the right as she disappeared. The act seemed strange at first, but I realized to onlookers, she seemed to have gotten lost in the crowd.

Wolf glanced over to me as we walked. "The lady's gotta a nice trick there."

"I'm just glad she doesn't get to Nashville often. Santini would blow a gasket trying to figure out how shit was being lifted," I muttered, thinking about my friend on the Nashville Police force.

The diner, as it turned out, was the same one I'd had breakfast at earlier. We shrugged and left the heat rising from the sidewalk, entering the cooler restaurant. The woman behind the counter gave a half-hearted smile and waved to a group of empty booths along the front windows.

"Coffee?" she asked.

"Three. We have someone joining us shortly," I replied, and slid into the same booth I'd eaten at earlier. Wolf sat across from me, nervously tapping his fingers on the table.

"You okay?"

"Long story," he said.

A few men sat at the far end of the counter, looking disapprovingly at the black man and myself. Smiling, I tipped my hat at them. Most places like this were *Whites Only,* but I didn't see a sign out front.

While the men's attention seemed focused on us, they didn't spot the sudden appearance of Luna behind them. The clever witch strolled by them, surprising them. Their eyes didn't leave her until she slid into the booth beside me.

"Introductions?" When neither said a word, I took it on myself to get the ball rolling. "Thomas Dietrich. On vacation from Nashville."

Luna tilted her head, looking surprised. "The Dietrich? The vampire slayer? The one from the war?"

I nodded. Apparently, you kill a few monsters and suddenly everyone knows your name.

"I read about you in that book," Luna said.

My eyes opened a bit wider. "Book?"

"The Monster Hunter," Wolf added.

"Yes. That's the one. Written by the same guy who did the one about UFO's," Luna said, smiling. "Never met anyone with a whole book about him."

I swear, I felt my jaw hitting the floor. Monsters and such were known about but rarely reported on in the media. The Feds and local governments liked to keep the population in the dark about what's really going on out there.

"What? Wait, when did this come out?" I asked, frantically.

"Last month," they said together.

"Tells all about you hunting vampires and werewolves in Nashville and how you put down some major badass in the Pacific during the war. Most people would chalk it up to conspiracy theorist bullshit, but I know better," Luna said, grinning from ear to ear.

I couldn't help but sigh. A book about me was all I needed. A fair share of reporters in Nashville had questioned me from time to time, but I wasn't aware of anyone who could have written a book.

"And your connection to Barkley?" Luna asked, flatly.

I paused as the waitress came around with three cups of coffee and a small tray with sugar and creamer. She placed it the table and quickly scribbled down our orders, a burger and fries for each of us. Once she'd left, I started to answer, but didn't get a chance.

Luna tilted her head as she looked at me with a knowing look. "Let me guess, you sold your soul to bed some super-hot dame, right?"

"Not exactly. My girlfriend did. We were both a little too drunk to catch on to what was really happening." I shook my head.

"Your girlfriend wanted to bed a super-hot dame?" Luna asked, and her eyes widened as I nodded. "I like her already."

Looking to Wolf, I asked, "And you?"

"A client's teenage son got caught up in some voodoo crap. He's only seventeen, but Barkley has a mortgage against his soul and this is my only way to save him," Wolf said, reaching for the creamer. "We all have a reason for needing the penny, but only one of us can return it to Barkley. But… it sounds like we should work together."

He poured some into his coffee and then offered it to Luna.

She leaned over the table, letting the steam from mug waft upwards, encircling her head like a halo. When she spoke, her words came out more like purring instead of the sarcastic tone she'd taken with me. "I prefer it black, like most things in my life."

"I'm curious, Mr. Wolf, where is home? You'd mentioned something about being brought to this city." I asked.

He looked at me. "From Charleston, South Carolina. I'm a Private Investigator and occasional hunter of the undead. Being in that line of work, I've heard all manner of stories about you and your exploits around Nashville, even before reading the book."

I gave a nod of appreciation.

His expression darkened "About that. The book, I mean. I know about your deeds in the Pacific. What you fought and what you sacrificed. Decorated by the President for your resourcefulness and skill. Or, should we just put it down to luck? I mean, the book tells a lot but not exact how you killed the Kwenta behemoth."

"It's hard to explain," I whispered, and hoped to change the topic.

Wolf nodded and continued. "I was in Japan after the bombs were dropped. Tales of what happened and what you did were a little more specific. Well, until the U.S. clamped down on what was reported in their papers."

Luna glanced back and forth. "A medal?"

"Mother fucking Medal of Honor," Wolf whispered into his coffee.

My mind touched on the image of the medal and the light blue ribbon it hung from, boxed up and sitting in a drawer at home. Hidden away like an unwanted memory. A chunk of shiny brass and gold. A trinket for killing the unkillable and for having the mental fortitude not to have lost my mind in the process.

Luna turned, her mouth opened in surprise. "No kidding? What the hell did you do? I read the book. They said the witnesses claimed it was as big as a mountain."

I didn't speak, but Wolf looked at me, and I could read his expression. He knew it wasn't something I wanted to discuss. So he answered for me. "Let's just say he fought a monster and…" he paused and looked into my sad eyes. He sighed, giving me a knowing tilt of the head. "Did what had to be done."

An awkward silence fell over the group until Luna spoke again.

"So Nashville?"

"Yep. Nashville was built atop one of the thirteen doorways to Hell. So, all manner of unholy shit keeps popping up there. It's a hub for the Vampire Cartel. Home to one of the largest werewolf clans in the Southeast, and the cultists—all the fucking cultists."

Wolf sipped his coffee before continuing. "So, I'm a bit out of my element here. You're from Nashville, and I'm guessing the lovely is from out of town too. We're all in the same boat. Strangers walking strange streets, looking for a dame and a coin."

Luna leaned on her elbows and looked back and forth between us. "Chicago. I'm from Chicago."

"And that trick?" Wolf asked.

I responded before she could answer. "Witchcraft. She's a spell-slinger. I've seen the trick before. Just never seen it used quite like that. In fact, I've never seen anyone quite so adept at casting a spell without an elaborate ceremony or some sort of offering. No circle or anything beforehand."

"I prefer the term Neo-Sorceress. Spell-slinger sounds so generic, and witch sounds so eighteenth century," Luna said nonchalantly.

I laughed. "But aside from that, you're just a run of the mill cat burglar."

Smiling, she nodded. "I prefer the term, Acquirer of Unobtainable Goods. I can turn invisible, along with anything I'm holding or wearing. Takes a little more concentration, but that's my specialty. Took me years to perfect the right combination of magic words and sounds to make it just so." She glared at me. "You know, today is the first time anyone has ever caught me. Hell, the first time anyone even knew I was in the same room with them."

"Wanna know my trick?" I asked, and her eyes open a little wider. I tapped the side of my nose. "Your perfume. I remembered it from our earlier encounter on the street earlier."

She shook her head, "That won't happen again."

"Tabu Forbidden. It's my girl's favorite brand. I know it well," I said with a smile.

She scoffed then looked at Wolf and smiled again. "What kinda powers you got, big boy?"

"Strength. Always had muscles, and I work on building them, daily. Trained in martial arts in Japan after the war. Just always been a little faster and stronger than everyone else. Family secret is that my mother paid a white witch to bless me, right after I was born. That and I've got a lot up here." He tapped his temple. "I've studied enough to know how people, alive or undead, think."

I grabbed the sugar and poured a small measure into my coffee and then I also offered it to Luna.

"I like my coffee like my men, hot, black, and stronger than usual." This time, she looked straight at Wolf, her eyes half lidded.

Shifting in his seat and looking uncomfortable, Wolf blushed and replied, "I have a fiancée, back home."

Without missing a beat, she purred back, "Did I say I was looking for a commitment?"

"So," I started, trying to bring the conversation back to another topic. "Do we battle one another or team up and find the damn penny?"

Reluctantly, they nodded. I filled them in on what I'd learned about Margo and her new railroad tycoon husband from Miss Eva and Ginger.

"We still have another player in the game," Luna said, and I heard the concern in her tone. "The other demon, Barbas."

"Barkley told you about him?" I asked and watched as they nodded.

"I can handle him," Wolf said, cracking his knuckles.

"Think brute strength will win the day?" I asked.

He held up both hands, wiggling his fingers and drawing attention to the two gold rings, one on each hand. Deep enameled lines and ancient-looking symbols were carved into the metal. It reeked of some sort of strange power. Something told me they weren't something you'd find at a typical jewelry store.

"That much gold could set someone up, pretty nicely for a year or two." Luna said, leaning out over the table towards him.

"Some kind of holy trinket?" I asked. Wolf smiled and winked.

"We still need a plan. I know where Bernard Bentington lives. I've already scoped the place out this morning but didn't see anything special or any sign of Margo," Luna explained.

"How long have you both been in town?" I asked, wondering how she already knew so much about Margo's whereabouts.

The waitress returned and deposited three plates in front of us. The burgers were smaller than I'd have liked but the fries were thick and meaty, just like I like them.

Luna answered, "I got here yesterday morning. I lucked out and saw an article in the social pages about Bentington's sudden engagement to the lovely Miss Margo. It didn't take too much effort to find out where his castle is. I dropped in late last night and did a bit of snooping around but came up empty."

"I got here around midnight, last night," Wolf said in between bites of his burger. "Went by the club, after hours, and saw a big ass demon that I'm pretty sure is Barbas and his boys leaving."

"How did you know it was him?" Luna asked.

"Apparently, there's something about these holy rings that allows me to see through his illusions. See, he and his demons make themselves look like regular folks." He tapped a finger just below his right eye. "But, these peepers with these rings can see them for what they are. When my jaw hit the ground, Barbas realized I was a danger."

Luna, hanging on every word, asked, "And what did you do? Demonic throw-down in the wee-hours of the night?"

"Pretty much. He had three lesser demons with him. They dropped fast. Barbas, if it was him, didn't go down. I held my own against him before more demons arrived to assist him in getting away." Wolf hesitated before speaking again. "Know how the bad guys always love to monologue when they think they have the upper hand? Telling you too much in the process? He let me know about Margo and her new man. Seems the penny is well hidden from him too. Seems that he should be able to track it down, know where it's at, but something is keeping it from his sight. I've never met Margo but the dame had enough smarts to figure out how to hide it from him."

I tapped my fingers on the table as I thought out loud. "I don't think she came up with it. Whatever the trick is, I suspect it's passed from person to person along with the coin. The penny has gone through a number of hands before Margo's and he's not found it yet."

"So where does that leave us to look?" Luna asked.

I sipped my coffee and thought about it.

"She has to have it on her. Maybe wearing it as a charm or hiding it in her shoe or purse," Luna said.

"I think the real question may be what's hiding it from Barbas's sight? If he created the damn thing and imbued it with his power, he should be able to see it, sense it, or whatever." I took a bite of my burger and let possibilities roll through my thoughts.

"Ma'am, do you have a copy of today's social pages?" Luna called out to the waitress.

The waitress walked to the counter and pulled out a section. Turning, she placed it and our check on the table. "Here ya go, hun,"

"We should hit the streets," I said.

"Got an idea?" Luna asked.

"Maybe." I pulled a wad of bills from my pocket and tossed a few on the table. Luna and Wolf stood and proceeded out the door without uttering a word.

I tipped my hat towards the waitress. "Compliments to the chef. That was some good eats."

Eleven

"We're running out of time and places to look," Luna huffed as she plopped down on a bench, a block away from the diner.

"Don't worry. There is a world of places to look." Wolf smiled reassuringly, but Luna wasn't having any of it.

"I'm not a detective. I steal things, I don't snoop around, digging up clues, and telling folks I'll find their lost trinkets or loved ones." She crossed her arms and stared off into the distance, still holding the crumpled Society pages in her hand.

"Sometimes, all it takes is looking at what's in front of you," I said.

She gave me a quizzical look, and I motioned to the paper. Her eyes glanced at the folded social pages then slowly looked back up to meet my gaze. A playful expression appeared as she unfolded the newsprint and started reading.

"Are you making fun of me, Mr. Dietrich?" she asked in an upbeat manner.

Her smile and wide eyes rattled me as she looked up. For just a brief moment, I saw Natalie sitting there. The face I adored, grinning in that cheerful way that'd become a standard for her when we are together.

Clearing my throat and returning to the moment, I answered. "It's easy to get distracted when the fight or the search is personal."

A few folks walked by us, women mostly, whispering back and forth about the snug catsuit Luna wore. The word *scandalous* wafted through the air. Meanwhile the few men that passed us, all gave side-glances at Wolf and muttered to themselves.

"Ideas?" Wolf asked.

"Margo is Bentington's arm candy now, bought and paid for. My guess is that she has him out shopping for goodies, maybe even arranging the wedding plans," I responded.

Wolf laughed. "Ever thought they could have snuck off for a romp in the hay in some secluded hideaway?"

"Oh God…" Luna groaned. "I just saw a picture

of Bernard Bentington. Old and wrinkled. Last thing I needed is the mental image of them going at it like rabbits."

Wolf and I couldn't help but laugh for a moment until we had the same mental images.

"Where? Where would they go if they wanted a secluded sex lounge?" I asked.

Wolf shook his head and Luna did the same when I looked to her. Then Wolf's face lit up.

"We need information and I think I have a source," Wolf said.

I gave him a puzzled look, so he pointed across the street. Luna and I huffed in agreement when we saw the shoeshine stand.

"You're kidding, right?" Luna asked.

Moments later, we were across the street and approaching the shoe shiner.

"Another shine already?" a young black man asked Wolf as we approached.

"Spent a hard day wearing down the last one," Wolf said, and nodded to the building behind us.

An awning overhanging an open window, advertised hot dogs for sale. A greasy man stood just inside it, nodding and giving us a welcoming expression. His finger pointed to a sign, *3 dogs for 50 cents.*

Despite his size, Wolf fit in the shoe shiner's chair and placed a foot on the stand. He checked his watch and leaned back as if he didn't have a care in the world. Without a word between them, the young man began applying polish with a small brush to Wolf's shoe.

"Wanna get some dogs?" Wolf looked at me, and I shook my head.

"We just ate. You can't possibly be hungry again, can you?" I said.

He laughed and shook his head. "No. I mean, it's almost top of the hour. News'll be on shortly. Buy me a dog and hang close to the radio to see if the local news cats give our boy Bentington a shout out."

Turning, I faintly heard Nat King Cole singing *Mona Lisa* in between the noise of passing cars. A radio sat on the hot dog seller's counter. It was then that I realized why the seller was nodding. It was in time to the music.

Stepping a little closer, I held up a single finger and then changed to three. "One dog, three sodas."

Wolf shouted back over his shoulder, "Load it down with some mustard."

I paid and looked around as Wolf turned his attention to Luna.

"I've found that sometimes kids like this are the

best ways to pick up what's happening on the street." Wolf spoke softly.

The young man looked up, smiling and nodding.

"And your shoes are looking spiffy," Luna said as she walked behind him, running her nails along the back of his neck. "You'd be surprised how many ladies appraise a man from the ground up. You know what they say about the size of a man's foot, don't you?"

Wolf cleared his throat. "Did I mention my fiancée, back home?"

She ran a hand under his chin and lifted it so she could look down into his eyes. "Hun, when you're two states away, I think it's okay."

I cleared my throat. "Jesus, get a room."

Everyone looked to me, and I suddenly felt very uncomfortable. Realizing I should have kept my mouth shut, I tried getting things back on course. I pulled a bill from my pocket and held it out to Wolf, who in turn handed it the young shoe shiner.

"Heard any scuttlebutt about Bernard Bentington, this morning?" Wolf asked in a low voice.

"They got hitched a little while ago. Just before lunch." The shiner looked up and pointed back to the radio. "The news reporter came on a while ago and announced they up and married at the courthouse. The whole city is buzzing about it."

Luna cocked and eyebrow. "The dame works fast."

"I wonder who his lawyer is," I muttered, and everyone turned to give me questioning looks. "If she works that fast, who's to say she hasn't conned the old boy into changing his will. You know she'll wanna make sure she gets everything."

All eyes turned to the shoe shiner.

"Don't be looking at me. That sort of info is out of my league."

I couldn't help but laugh, but the amusement was short lived.

Wolf had been right. Cole finished his crooning on the airways, which led straight into a news update.

"And in local news, Bernard Bentington, famed railroad industrialist and Memphis native, was married this morning in a surprise ceremony at the Shelby County courthouse by a Justice of the Peace. The new bride, a local girl named Margo Posten, has reportedly only been seeing Mr. Bentington for a few weeks, but this goes to show how fast love can work."

"It wasn't love that got him to move that fast," I muttered.

"The penny or her kitty?" Wolf asked.

Luna smirked. "I'd say both."

The announcer continued with some background on Bentington.

"Our sources tell us that friends of the tycoon will be throwing a party this evening in the swanky Butler Building, a congratulations to the new couple before they are whisked off to some undisclosed honeymoon destination."

We looked at one another as the sports announcer began rambling out scores. If she were married, it meant getting close to her would be more difficult. Plus, if she and the new husband decided to leave early for their honeymoon, we'd be stuck without a way to track her down in time to meet the return deadline.

The young man tossed his polishing rag aside and clapped his hands. "All done, sir."

Wolf stood, admiring the gleam from the shining leather. "The man said the Butler Building. I suggest we head over there."

"Order up!" The vendor placed the hot dog and bottles on the counter.

"And get a lay of the land, so to speak. We know she'll be there, eventually," Luna said and picked up her soda.

I looked around, and the towering Hotel Tennessee caught my eye. A sudden feeling of loneliness and dread washed over me. In a darkened room, in a soft bed, wrapped in an evil cocoon of sleep and blankets lay my princess. Her future rested in my hands and all I had were thin leads and quickly dissolving hopes.

The others needed the penny as much as I did. A life or a soul was at stake for each of us. When we got the coin, then what? Would we turn on each other? I could beat Luna. That much I was sure of, but Wolf had the speed and muscle of the fiercest monsters I'd ever faced. And, as much as I loved Natalie and needed her safe, they'd be fighting just as hard for their own reasons.

"Luna can get inside, maybe draw up a map or something," Wolf said, and crammed the hot dog into his mouth.

"Luna, if you can do that, we might just get the upper hand on Margo. I'm going to take a chance and see if I can find his lawyer," I said, looking at the two. "If luck is on her side, she really may have talked the old boy into changing his will before the honeymoon. Maybe I can catch them there. It's worth a shot."

They looked at one another and then back to me. Wolf nodded, accepting the plan, but Luna narrowed her eyes, and I could understand her suspicions.

Holding up a hand, I gave the time-honored Boy Scout salute.

"Scout's honor. If I see them, I won't take the penny for myself. We all have a stake in this and one way or another, we'll all win. Meet me outside the Hotel Tennessee in a couple of hours."

Twelve

A short time later, I opened the door to my room at the Hotel Tennessee. The air inside felt thick, like the place had been sealed for a thousand years. On the bed, right where I'd left her, lay Natalie.

Pulling off my hat and jacket and tossing them on a nearby chair, I crossed the room, sat beside her and leaned close. The smell of her perfume had faded overnight, but enough remained to bring a smile to my face. The scent of sex still lingered too, but that did nothing for me now. I had more important thoughts running through my head.

I pressed my lips to her temple and kissed the slumbering angel. A tremor shot through my hand as I ran my fingers through her blonde curls. My heart raced as I thought of failure.

No. I couldn't let her down.

Thirty minutes later, I hung up the phone after exhausting my list of contacts in town. Memphis wasn't home, but at least I knew enough people here to make the effort worth a try. Still, no one had a clue about who Bentington's lawyers might be or his whereabouts.

Miss Eva came to mind. Asking her for assistance was out of the question, albeit it with her connections, I'd wager that she already had the answer. Then a thought struck. She'd mentioned wanting to work with Lily, work with Voodoo Rumors. Maybe...

Pulling out my wallet, I rummaged through it until I found the card I needed. Picking up the phone, I asked the hotel's operator to place a long-distance call to Nashville.

A wave of relief hit me as a familiar female voice answered.

"This is the law firm of Joseph McElroy. How may I assist you?"

"Dottie? This is Thomas Dietrich," I said quickly.

"Dietrich? I can barely hear you," she replied in a soft voice.

My voice rose as I spoke again. "Listen, I need to call in a favor."

Over the years, Joseph and his secretary, Dottie had assisted me in a number of legal matters. His law firm specialized in paranormal cases. As such, we'd worked hand in hand many times.

I heard a snicker. "Calling in one of mine or one the boss's favors?"

"Either or both. I don't care which. I need to know what attorney or law firm in Memphis handles Bernard Bentington, the railroad tycoon."

The pause seemed to last an eternity. Then she spoke again. "Thomas, that kind of info is confidential, but I'll make some calls. But... umm... I'd like dinner. There is a new steakhouse, downtown. You know, that fancy joint in your neck of the woods. They've got a five-dollar steak that is supposed to melt in your mouth."

I sighed, "You know I've got a girlfriend, right?"

Laughter erupted from the receiver, causing me to hold the phone away from my ear for a moment.

"I know, silly. I'm not looking to jump you. I just want a steak dinner. Bring her along for all I care. Now, let me call some friends. How can I get back in touch with you?"

I looked at the phone and gave her the hotel's number and my room information.

"This shouldn't take long, I'll call back in a bit," she said, just as the line clicked dead.

I placed the receiver down and my hand hovered over the phone as one bad idea after another shot through my thoughts. I glanced to Natalie and curse myself for letting this happen to her.

Balling up my fists, I stepped to the window and opened the drapes. The afternoon sunlight flooded the dark room, which felt more like a tomb with every passing second.

I heard an exaggerated grunt behind me. Spinning, I found Barkley, sitting on the bed, running his fingers through Natalie's golden curls.

"Can't you warn a guy when you're going to do something like that?" he moaned, blinking. "Ever thought that perhaps a demon may not care for that much sunlight?"

Without thinking, I crossed the room, grabbed the suited demon by the lapels, lifted him up, and slammed him backwards into the wall. The thud of his skull against plaster warmed my heart.

"Keep your hands off her!"

He rolled his head forward and looked at me. A sinister grin curled across his face. I let him go and took a step back. Twisting his head and cracking his neck a couple of times, he straightened his jacket. A low chuckle boiled up from within him.

He smacked his lips and gave me an unnerving look. "If it offers you some measure of encouragement to return what was lost, when she is taken to, what Dante referred to as the Second Ring, I plan on being the first of an endless string of demons to sample her."

Heat crawled up my face, and I saw delight in Barkley's eyes at that.

"Go on, Thomas. Let the evil part of you take over," he hissed. "You can kill me, but I won't die. But wouldn't it make you feel so much better to pummel me? Maybe a bullet through my skull? What's a few more black spots in the Father's Book of Life to a man like you?"

I wanted to grab my pistol and blow his head off, but he was right. It'd do me no good. Taking a deep breath and pushing the anger away, I felt my blood pressure drop. When my eyes reopened, Barkley's grin had faded into a frown.

"I'm not evil," I said softly.

He scoffed and looked at Natalie. "How many men have you killed? How many monsters? How many times have you let your anger get the better of you? You're a human; it's what you do. The Father designed you to have an evil side. The trick for you humans to figure out is whether or not you can learn to control it."

"Bullshit." I stepped closer to Natalie.

"You think your… sweetheart is so innocent? A stripper and newly-minted hooker when you met her. So ready to sell herself to whatever man offered her some cash. And now stripping as her night job? You know she loves dancing, loves showing herself to men. Knowing that every man in the joint is looking at those big bouncing tits and jiggling ass. All that attention makes her nether regions tingle with delight. And when she comes to your apartment, after you've both been working all evening, it isn't you that has her wet and ready. No, Thomas. She spends her nights loving the attention, letting all the strangers get her revved up, and then jumps on you and grinds in order to get the release."

Biting my lip and keeping my rage under control, my brain plotted out the top ten ways to punch the bastard, ensuring the optimal effect and damage.

"Her lust, her deviant needs are what brought you to this point, isn't it?" he said as his smile grew.

Barkley shook his head. "She's well on her way to being as deviant as your sister, and we both know I'm aware of Lily's lustful wants, the dancers she takes to bed each night for more than just sleep."

"What's the point of bringing this up? Are you trying to convince me of something? Make me angry enough to kill you?" I bit off each word as I spoke, crossing my arms and staring the demon down.

"I'm merely poking the dragon, my boy. I need the penny, and I need you to get it. But that doesn't mean I can't have a little fun, along the way." He pulled a cigarette from his jacket and lit it from a flame emanating from his finger.

"I'm tired of dealing with you. We have a deal in place, now stay out of my way." My anger seeped into the words as I spoke.

"You thought about the others? Wolf and Lavender? Plan on killing them for the penny when you find it?" he asked.

"When the time comes, I'll do what I need to do."

He blew a puff of smoke in my face and watched the gray coils swirl for a moment.

"Whoever puts the coin in my hand, wins. Simple as that, Thomas. For her sake, you'd better make sure it's you."

The phone rang, drawing our attention away from one another. Stepping fast, I snatched up the receiver.

"Dietrich here."

Dottie's voice made my heart stop, but just for a moment. "Thomas, Edward Palmer of Palmer, Jenkins, and Woodard. That's who you want to find."

Grabbing a pencil and notepad, I scribbled out the information as Dottie repeated it. Looking up at Barkley as I finished the call, he gave a nod and tapped his watch. He raised a hand. With a slight twist of his wrist, the whole of reality seemed to fracture and shift to the side.

And he was gone, leaving only the telltale wisps

of cigarette smoke in his wake. I stood there for a moment, thinking about what he'd said. A kernel of an idea began to form, something that might put the damn demon in his place.

Sitting down beside Natalie again and leaning forward, I pressed my mouth pressed against her ruby-colored lips. My fingers tousled her curls, and I remembered the first time I'd done it.

"I don't know if you can hear me. Just know that no matter what, I love you and I will never stop fighting to keep you at my side."

One more kiss and I headed for the door.

Thirteen

Leaving the hotel, I snagged one of the bright yellow cabs, lined up and down the block. Luckily, the cabbie knew exactly where the law firm of Palmer, Jenkins, and Woodard was located. I waved a five-dollar bill at him and told him to stomp the gas and ignore the reds. He earned the tip.

I could have taken my Studebaker but not knowing the roads and being forced to rely on a map would have cost me precious time. Not to mention finding a parking spot in the city would be a major pain in the ass.

"Here we are, sir. The Central Bank Building," the cabbie announced.

A couple of blocks away, the sign on another tower grabbed my attention.

"Butler Building," I muttered, remembering that was the place where the big shindig would be taking place.

Stepping out onto the busy sidewalk, I briefly took in the view of the towering structure and those around it. Although impressively built, the buildings couldn't keep my attention for very long as my eyes were immediately pulled back to street level when I heard voices calling out.

A crowd of reporters and on-lookers had assembled around the entranceway of the Central Bank Building. Like a swarm of angry bees, reporters and photographers called out questions as a couple emerged from the building. I could only get a brief glimpse or two, but it was obvious who the couple was: Mr. Bentington and his new bride, Margo.

As they slid into a waiting limo, a short, plump woman emerged from the building, racing through the converging crowd with an envelope in her hand and determination in her eyes.

"Mr. Bentington, wait! You forgot to sign! Make way, please." She pushed her way through the sea of humanity surrounding the couple's car, momentarily disappearing from my sight.

I pushed my way closer, trying to listen.

The driver, who'd almost closed the door, must have heard her pleas because he reopened it to allow the woman to hand the brown file folder to the old man. I could just make out an old man, appearing to scribble something, then closed the folder and handed it back to her. With that done, the door closed, sealing the couple away from the excited onlookers.

I tried to get closer, but before I could, the limo drove off. Turning back around, I saw my cab had already pulled away, just disappearing into downtown traffic. Raising my hand to hail another cab, my heart sank as no others appeared. I considered running after the limo, but in the end, I just watched it disappear around a corner.

So damn close and yet, nothing. In frustration, I glanced around, trying to think of something I could do. And then I saw her, the young, plump woman re-entering the Central Bank Building. She must work for the lawyer. Maybe she knew where they were heading. It was worth a try if I could get an opportunity to talk to her.

Darting through the dispersing crowd, I charged through the doors. On the far side of the lobby, the woman had just stepped into an elevator. I broke into a sprint. My footfalls echoed through the lobby, their tempo matching my heartbeat. With a last second leap, I barely made it inside before the doors closed.

"You're in a hurry," she said, leaning in front of me and pushing the button for the twelfth floor.

She had a warm smile and friendly demeanor. Smartly dressed, her thick glasses, pixie-cut hair, and professional stance suggested paralegal.

Thinking quickly, I came up with a story. I extended my hand to the panel and hesitated before pushing one.

"Oh, we're going to the same floor. Sorry if I'm out of breath. Trying to catch Mr. Bentington before he leaves. His people called me this morning to make arrangements for a last-minute trip. A honeymoon, I think, but none of them could give me any details on where the couple would like to visit. I've got to track him down, so I can get their travel arrangements in order."

The woman tilted her head and smiled. "I'm so sorry. You just missed him. They left in their limo, a few minutes ago. Didn't you see it out there?"

I feigned surprise. "What? Damn. Oh, pardon me. I saw one but didn't realize it was them. His people told me he was going to be here, making changes to his will."

I threw it out there, the suspicion I'd had. She confirmed my thoughts with a roll of her eyes. Then she held up the folder and snickered.

"Mrs. Bentington was so concerned about tonight's party; she didn't let him stay long enough to sign the copy." She shook the folder then dropped her hand to her side. "Luckily, I caught him in time. For all the good that does."

My eyes followed the brown folder. The unbound papers within it, slipped and were exposed out of the bottom by a half an inch.

I looked back into her eyes and gave a halfhearted smile. "I take it that you disapprove?"

"Not my place to say." She looked away.

"I think we all know that Mr. Bentington's new dame is, or was a performer at the Golden Rhino," I said, hoping for a reaction and was rewarded with a generous nod.

"From what I know of the place, the clientele is composed of wealthy and powerful men. Politicians, businessmen, and I'd bet some of your firm's partners are regulars at that place," I said and waited. A moment later, I was again rewarded with a sigh and a nod.

She turned and looked at me. Her voice was low but had a sharp edge to it. "For the past couple of weeks, ever since it became common knowledge that Bentington had started dating her, the partners have been talking up a storm. Gossiping like a flock of old women, if you ask me."

"Oh? What do they say?" I asked innocently. When she didn't answer, I added, "Sometimes, a stranger is the best person to talk to." I smiled and extended my hand. "Thomas."

"Mattie."

"So, Margo being a Rhino girl bothers you?" I asked.

"Yes. Mr. Bentington has always been a sweet man to me when he comes in for business. Don't get me wrong, if she makes him happy, great." She forced a smile as the elevator stopped and the door slid open.

"No point in me getting off here. I'll head back down," I said, and shuffled a bit closer to her as I extended my hand again.

She took my hand, looked up, and smiled. "Thank you. Look, I shouldn't say this, but Mrs. Bentington kept insisting that they go to the hotel and pick up a few things. Maybe you can catch them there, depending on what hotel she's talking about."

"Hotel?" I asked. I would have thought Bentington would be staying in his home but then I slapped my forehead as the realization hit me. The hotel by the Rhino. Where her room is.

"Thank you for that," I said.

As she turned to go, I lowered my hand and pinched the papers between my fingers. Mattie walked off, not noticing as the copy of the will, slid out of the folder. Once clear, I pulled my hand with the will behind my back and pushed the button for the ground floor with my free hand.

The hum of the machinery relaxed me as I quickly scanned the document. The will was several pages long, but the first couple of pages indicated the gist of the changes. While Bentington's vast railroad and other corporate holdings were promised to his children, all the money, stocks, and other financial holdings were now going to Margo. If the old man died tomorrow, she could easily be the richest woman in the state, if not the richest, this side of the Mississippi.

The doors slid open, and I briskly walked to a guard's desk, positioned along the side wall. The young man with a worthless badge looked up at me.

"You have a phone?" I asked. He nodded, so I continued. "Can you call the law firm upstairs? Ask for Mattie. Tell her she dropped something in the elevator."

I folded the papers in half and waited as he made the call. The thought of leaving the will with the guard occurred to me, but if her employers discovered a prize client's new will had been exposed or lost, she'd be fire without a second thought,

It didn't take long before I saw her bound out of the elevator, like a prized racehorse, leaving the gate at Churchill Downs. Her panicked face turned to one of joy and gratitude as she approached and took the will from my outstretched hand.

A while later, I rounded a corner and stopped a block from the Rhino and its companion hotel. The streets were clogged with cars, seemingly moving only a few feet at a time before stopping for extended periods. The sidewalks hosted a few folks, here and there, but no one took any notice of me. Hopping onto a bench, I looked over the unmoving parade of automobiles, but there wasn't any sign of the black limo parked near the hotel.

More importantly, the Rhino didn't appear to have beefed up security since my last appearance around here. I'd expected an army, or at least a few extra men at the doors. I looked to the roof and there they were. Six men, at least, walking about and keeping an eye on things below. A pair of them carried hunting rifles, and from their perches, they could make short work of anyone causing trouble. But I could use their disadvantage to my favor. One man from that distance looks like any other. They would see me and not realize I posed a threat.

Then a thought struck me. What if Miss Eva and her boys were out looking for Margo as well? Surely, they'd know about the party tonight, where the new couple were supposed to be the honored guests.

I needed to get back into Margo's old apartment, to see if she had been there and what she may have taken. Knowing might give me an idea of what to look for later, the special hiding place that kept the penny from demon eyes.

A direct approach, walking up and going straight inside, wouldn't work, and there wasn't time to get another gold token. Even if there was, the guard or doorman might be on the lookout for me or Wolf.

A split-second before I was going to step off the bench, a navy-blue Ford Deluxe pulled to a stop in front of the hotel. The driver laid on the horn for a minute before a blond man emerged, strolling to the vehicle. Regardless of the distance between us, the man's size looked unnaturally large and well defined.

"Well that's new. Is that Barbas?" I whispered.

The man, wearing a white suit, slid into the car's passenger seat. With a roar, the car pulled into traffic and turned, making a U-turn and jetting away down a side street, in the opposite direction.

Since no one around the Rhino and hotel seemed concerned, I sprinted, weaving through the unmoving cars. Getting closer, I could see the doorman from earlier, slumped down in the corner of the hotel's lobby, out of sight from the sidewalk and bleeding from a wound on his head.

"Sorry, brother. I need to check on the girls and

make sure they're okay," I blurted out.

Not bothering to stop, I ran past him and charged up the stairs to the second floor. As soon as I stepped into the hallway, several sets of eyes turned to stare at me. The women were standing in the corridor and talking at once, concern painted across their faces. Worse yet, they were all crowded around Ginger's doorway.

"What happened here?" I asked. "Everyone okay?"

"A big guy bashed his way in here, slapped Gin around pretty good," a brunette said, eyeing me suspiciously.

A blonde spoke up. "Knocked down Margo's door and tore the place up. Kept saying he couldn't find it. Not sure what he was looking for."

I heard the sultry voice of Ginger answer. "He wanted Margo and her lucky penny. Bet it's the same thing she was bragging about."

She staggered into the hallway, supported on either side by her sisters. The right side of her face appeared red and swollen in the dim lights. He'd roughed her up a good bit. Ginger's eyes met mine, and she gave a halfhearted smile.

"Hiya, handsome. Not how I thought I'd be seeing you again."

"I'm sorry this happened," I said. "You shouldn't

have gotten caught up in any of this. None of you should have. Did he say anything about Margo?"

She shook her head, wincing from the pain. "No. Just that he wanted the penny back. Missed Margo by fifteen minutes. She ran in long enough to grab some clothes, a couple of books, and her Bible. Said she was going back to the house to put on the new threads from her hubby. Then they'd be heading to the big shindig. They're leaving for the honeymoon tomorrow. I'm supposed to catch up with her tonight at the party."

She touched her face and hissed in pain. "I can't go like this. No one is gonna want to hook-up with a girl with a black eye."

The brunette, seeing my questioning expression, spoke up. "Miss Eva is furnishing entertainment for it."

"Of course, she is," I muttered.

I turned to leave, but Ginger called out to me. "Just keep Margo safe. She's my friend and she promised to find me a good man. She told us she's bringing her lucky penny tonight, so we can all make a wish on it."

"She said that?" I asked. "Okay, good to know. Thanks ladies."

Returning to the elevator, I noticed that the needle

on the floor indicator was moving from one to two. Security must be on their way up. Glancing around, I saw the sign for the stairway. Moving quickly, I opened the door and listened. No noise reached my ears, so I darted in and was on the ground floor in no time.

No one stood or moved in the lobby, so I started for the door. The doorman looked up at me and tried to speak. Changing course, I knelt beside him and pulled a handkerchief from my jacket. As I pushed the folded cloth against his head wound, he winced, but remained still. He didn't speak, but his eyes showed his appreciation.

"Hold this tight," I said. "When your buddies come back downstairs, have them get you to a hospital. That thing's gonna need stitches."

His shaking hand reached up and took the cloth, making him wince again.

"Thanks, brother," he whispered.

With that, I left and started walking for the Hotel Tennessee to meet up with my new friends. But first, I needed to go by the parking garage where my car sat. My monster hunting box lived in the trunk, and I wanted to grab a few things. All signs indicated we'd be going to war.

Fourteen

The long walk did me some good. It gave me time to digest what Ginger had said, or more specifically, the list of items that Margo had returned to claim. Grabbing some of her clothing and shoes seemed perfectly ordinary. A couple of books could mean a diary or something that had sentimental value, but her Bible. Now that got the wheels in my head turning.

I knew so little about Margo. Most women in her line of work aren't really the religious type, at least not the ones I've encountered. Maybe the Bible, like the books, had some intangible value or hope attached to it.

The fact that the demons couldn't find the penny, even though they'd made the damn thing, bothered me. The more I thought about how she'd hidden it, the more possibilities came to mind. Demons had powers and abilities, but they aren't all-powerful. Not even Barkley could see it. I'm sure if he could, the smug bastard would already have snatched it. Why involve us at all in that case?

I thought about the penny itself. Namely, the luck it gave to whoever owned it. I'd assumed that owning it meant carrying it with you all the time. But what if you didn't have to carry it around, like a lucky rabbit's foot or some other talisman? What if just being the owner of the thing was enough? Being able to hide it safely away while still enjoying the benefits would also explain a lot.

Margo had told the girls she'd bring the penny with her tonight. Question was, would it be the real coin or a fake in case there's trouble? I couldn't see her risking the penny by flaunting it in public.

I turned a corner and neared the hotel. The parking garage stood nearby. Surrounded by the smells of gasoline and motor exhaust, I headed in and climbed the spiraling concrete slope until I found my Studebaker.

Popping the trunk, I looked down at a large wooden box, specially made for me by my friends in Rome. Painted black and etched with runes from some language lost centuries ago, it stored my hunting gear. Dialing the combination into the lock, I heard the satisfying click as the last number slotted into place.

An empty leather carrying bag, which I kept conveniently next to the box, quickly reached its holding limit as I stuffed it full of my toys. Grabbing the bag, I closed the trunk lid and made my way out of the structure.

As I approached the Hotel Tennessee, I spotted Wolf pacing the sidewalk across the street. When he noticed me, I waved him over. Something seemed odd about the way he walked. As he got closer, I could tell why. He'd already stocked up on weapons.

Nothing showed, but his pistols were easy for a well-trained eye to spot. He packed a pair of shoulder holsters, one under each arm, exactly what I wore. I chuckled, remembering the old saying, great minds think alike.

"Where's Luna?" I asked and spun when I heard her voice.

"Right here. Can we go inside first? I'm not dressed for rush hour."

She was close enough that I felt her breath on my ear. A split second later, her perfume reached my nostrils, smothering the acidic stench of car exhaust from the passing traffic.

"Let's go up to my room. We can talk and plan out the evening in privacy," I said.

"Isn't your girl up there?" Luna's disembodied voice chimed.

I shrugged. "Umm. Yes, but I think she'll just sleep through it."

"Are we that boring?" Wolf quipped.

I shrugged again and sighed.

A few minutes later, I turned the key and opened the door to see my girl, still sleeping on bed. The curtains, still open from earlier, gave us plenty of light. The afternoon sun washed the walls and carpet in a brilliant yellow light.

A hint of sulfur wafted around us. I'd not noticed it earlier when Barkley was there, but then I had my mind focused on other things. Namely Natalie's safety.

I pointed to a table in the corner. "Have a seat. I'm gonna order up some room service. Pot of coffee and some sandwiches. Anyone want anything?"

Hearing some whispered words, I looked over in time to watch Luna fade back into sight. She dropped a red gown over the back of one of the chairs and placed a red pair of high heels and a matching clutch in the seat with it.

Wolf, who'd taken a seat at the table, was in the

right position to have full view of Luna's backside. His eyes studied her momentarily then looked in every other direction than hers.

"Coffee sounds good. Whiskey sounds better. All things considered, two pots of coffee, one bottle of bourbon, but make it something expensive. I'll cover it," Luna purred as she unbuckled her belt.

The woman dropped the belt next to her shoes and walked around, coming up behind Wolf. Laying her hands on his shoulders, she gave them a squeeze.

"Oh, hun. You're so tense. You need a woman's touch right about now."

Her hands began massaging, working and kneading his neck and shoulders. Wolf winced once or twice at first, appearing thoroughly uncomfortable. By the time I'd finished the room service order, he looked like he was in Heaven.

"Still engaged?" I joked.

Wolf snarled and sat up straight. Luna, taking the hint, stopped and walked over to the bed. Her head tilted as she looked at the sleeping beauty, then stooped down, lifting the edge of the covers and gazed at Natalie's face.

"Barkley has her in some kind of spell, called it a magical sleep. Said she'd stay that way until I get the penny," I said and stepped to the bed.

Luna smiled. "Looks like you two had good time.

Oh, wait. You said there was another woman. One that Barkley provided?"

I pushed her hand down, lowering the covers in the process.

She smiled and looked up at me. "Your Natalie is just a baby."

"She's twenty-five. Why does the age difference matter to everyone?" I growled.

"Twenty-five and you're—really old." Luna stood and gave me a playful elbow to the ribs as she walked past me. "Cradle-robber."

I sighed. "Is the age difference really that big a deal?"

Wolf snickered. "As long you love one another, no it doesn't."

We discussed plans, the building's layout, and what we expected to find, stopping briefly when the food arrived. Our manners went out the door as we grabbed up the bread, cold cuts, and drinks. In no time, we feasted like kings. The coffee helped with the exhaustion from a busy day of running about the city. The bourbon, an aged bottle of Colonel E.H. Taylor's finest, helped with everything else.

Luna unfolded a sheet a paper and dropped it on the table for us to examine. Her finger ran from one spot to another as she explained the Butler Building's floorplans, especially the area where the party was to take place and all the entrances and exits. Two stairwells and two elevators were the only ways in and out.

"There is a financial firm on the floor below and a law firm on the floor above. They both use the twenty-first floor as an open reception hall for swanky parties, meetings, and such," Luna explained.

"Ideas on how to get inside?" I asked before tilting my glass to get the last swallow of the Colonel's concoction in my gut.

"While no one was looking, I added our names to the guest list, so getting inside shouldn't be a problem. We'll just need to dress the part and act like we're better than regular folks." She looked at Wolf and smiled. "And since this is a pure white bread get-together, I listed you as a photographer with the local paper's social pages."

"I don't have a camera," Wolf growled.

Stepping to my suitcase, I pulled out my trusty Kodak and handed it over. "Just try not to break it, if a fight breaks out."

"If? No promises," he responded.

"What gear you taking inside?" he asked.

Grabbing my bag of toys. I placed it on the table and began to unpack; my trusty vampire-killing stake, silver push daggers, and several small vials of holy water. I unholstered my Colt automatic, and pulled a second one from the bag, along with a pair of smaller pistols.

"I have friends in Rome who always give me nice toys to play with. The stake is infused with holy water, engraved with something in Latin my priest says is like chili pepper to the eyes for a demon, and is heavily blessed, his words not mine. It's my favorite weapon to use against vampires, but it has its uses against demons of all sizes and all manner of unholy shit."

Wolf laid out his weapons: pistols, a polished bowie knife, and a wooden stake that'd been strapped to his right shin, under the pants leg. He also wiggled his fingers drawing attention to the rings.

He pointed to my pistols. "Silver bullets?"

I nodded and smiled as I piled up a handful of magazines for the weapons. Glancing to the side, I noticed Luna's expression darken.

"Luna, you have any weapons? Anything you usually carry to protect yourself?" I asked.

Looking over to me, she slowly shook her head. "Not to the extent that you're armed. I'm a thief. My game is avoiding fights. But I do have a little something."

Grabbing her clutch, she opened it but hesitated before pulling anything out.

"Okay, so I don't fight but I keep this with me all the time."

The switchblade popped open as soon as she brought it into view.

"You should carry something ranged, maybe a small pistol..." Wolf started but stopped when she inhaled suddenly.

Luna's tone was defiant as she spoke. "No. I don't like guns."

"I guess not. Don't really need them if you're trying to move about a place, without being seen or heard. Not wearing your catsuit into the party?" I pointed to the dress.

"No. I'd like to go in looking like a guest and see if I can cozy up to the other girls before they get a turn wishing on that penny. Maybe I can snag a place in line," she said.

"Sounds like a good idea. Look don't worry. Chances are, we'll get in and out of there without a problem. Stay close to Margo, just in case," I said, and then smiled as an idea came to me. "Since you're a thief, any skill at pickpocketing?"

She shrugged. "I'm okay. Being invisible does help, but my usual jobs are done when the rich folks are asleep, and the cops are bored."

I gave her a reassuring pat on the shoulder as we stood. I reached into my bag and pulled out a small pistol, a .25 automatic in a holster with an elastic strap. It'd been designed for a woman to wear on her thigh, under a skirt. I'd picked it up for Natalie, hoping that she'd never need it.

"I understand you don't like guns, but it'd make me feel better if you had something," I said, and watched her eyes focus on the petite weapon.

"I crap bigger things than that," Wolf laughed.

She and I rolled our eyes, but she snatched it from my hand and examined it. Pulling the gun from the holster, Luna held it in the palm of her hand, unsure of what to do next. I stepped closer, took it, and gave her a crash course in how to hold and use it safely.

"I should go ahead and get dressed." Luna grabbed the dress and headed for the bathroom.

She turned back to look us over. "When I'm done in here, you both should wash up and dress. I need you looking like you belong at a party like this. Rich men don't sweat and you two do, and the wealthy can spot undesirables like us a mile away.

As soon as the bathroom door closed behind her, Wolf frowned and whispered, "A little blade and a pop gun isn't gonna help her if the demons do show up."

"Demons? Oh, they'll be there, and I half expect Miss Eva and her boys to show up too. We're going into a war zone," I replied.

"Think she's up for this? This could be a shit-storm of Biblical proportions." He paused and pointed to the closed door. "And I'm not sure our thief is going to handle that too well."

"We've seen her in action. I think there is more to her than you realize. She can get close to Margo, and her invisibility can cover her if the danger level gets too high. War doesn't build character, it reveals it." I looked to the door and back to him. "I have no doubt that our character will be put to the test tonight."

Fifteen

We left at different times and took different routes to the Butler Building. Luna took a cab, while Wolf and I walked. Not that I thought anyone would notice, but you can't be too careful.

The humidity in the spring air felt cool against my face as I walked. The sun was down, and a thin sprinkle of stars glowed overhead, just visible through the haze which was illuminated by the electric lights of the city. Disappointment filled me at the sight. Everything man has created to benefit our measly existence on this rock has distorted something else. Artificial light has made the nighttime streets safer, but polluted the skies above, hiding God's heavens from our view. Perhaps the Amish or those other religious folks who see technology as evil are right.

Maybe when I retire from this life, I'll find a nice farm, way out in the country. Some place away from the city lights so Natalie and I can sit outside, watch the stars cross from horizon to horizon, and talk about our dreams and accomplishments.

My mind touched on Natalie and her dream as I rounded a corner and saw my destination a couple of blocks ahead of me. She wanted to be a singer. It's what had brought her to Nashville. If I got her home safe, I'd find a way to help her make that happen. Somehow, I'd do it for her.

The traffic in front of the building was bumper-to-bumper as limo after limo shuffled to get up close to the doorway. Bright lights flooded the entrance, and the crowd briefly turned stark white every few seconds as dozens of cameras clicked, firing off their flashbulbs.

I fell in with the well-dressed crowds as they entered the lobby. Near the elevators, a line had formed, and I could just make out the stunning figure of Luna. Gold adorned her neck and ears, and her hair fell down her back in loose curls.

The line moved quickly since many of the wealthy were apparently well known to the young man behind the check-in counter. In no time at all, I stepped up and smiled at the sharply dressed man, who looked me up and down.

"Name, sir?"

I smirked, pretending like he should know me.

"Dietrich. Thomas Dietrich. You must be new." I watched his finger run up and down the list. "Do you need me to spell it for you?"

He ignored me until his finger stopped near the end of the list.

"Yes, sir. Here we go. Please step into the elevators. The party is on the twenty-first floor," he said, and then looked past me to the next person in line.

"Thank you," I said, flashing a smile.

Stepping inside the metal cube, I wondered if it was safe for the elevator to carry this many people. I found myself pressed up against a couple of well-dressed gentlemen and their lovely young dates and an annoyed older man, whose Old Spice cologne competed to overpower all the other perfumes in the confined space. While I appreciated his attempt to cover up his smell, which it barely did, I had to wonder if the guy bathed in a tub of it. The faces of the folks around me told me I wasn't alone in this thought.

The random chitchat of the ladies and gents provided several moments of unexpected levity.

Trying not to smile, I glanced at my watch and then at the other passengers.

"Finally," one of the younger men said as we reached our destination.

The door slid open and revealed the opulent celebration for Memphis' newest married couple. Dozens of people already filled the vast, open floor. Unlike most of the other floors in the place, this one had only a few walled-off areas for storage and the men and women's facilities. Since the owners used this place for parties and events, I guessed there would be a kitchen somewhere behind the walls.

In the far-right corner sat a stage with a sizeable band playing some light jazz, which immediately had my toes metaphorically tapping. All around, folks danced, talked, and laughed. A full bar took up a portion of the left wall, and I spotted Luna, surveying the scene, perched on a stool already with a drink in her hand.

As I moved further into the place, I kept an eye on her. Within a space of five minutes, three different men approached her, did their best Valentino impersonations, and failed to solicit an invitation to stay.

Walking slowly, I mingled with as many people as I could, making small talk about the new couple, the local political scene, and whatever else these folks had to go on about. A couple of older men rambled on about the state of affairs in this country that'd allow a black man to be in a swanky place like this, even if he was there taking pictures for the papers.

Looking around, I spotted Wolf hamming it up with folks and getting mostly smiles as he clicked photo after photo. There'd be a bunch of pissed off people tomorrow wondering why their smiling faces aren't plastered on the pages of the social rags.

As the band, all dressed in matching red suits, finished up its rendition of *Star Dust*, a man's voice rang out, demanding attention and making every head turn towards the stage.

"Ladies and gentlemen, let me hear a round of applause for the band," the man on the stage said into the microphone.

The crowd showed their appreciation, and as the clapping died down, I spotted a couple approaching the stage. The blonde was all smiles as she whispered back and forth with the old man. I'd not seen a picture of either but had no doubts that this was Margo and her new husband. Both laughed and seemed genuinely happy, overjoyed to have found one another. They generated the kind of warm aura about themselves that tugged at the heartstrings of everyone watching.

Seeing them together, I wondered briefly if she

was truly happy, but experience in the P.I. game told me otherwise. I'd bet all the money in my pockets that the painted smile on the blonde's face was a well-acted fake. Deep down, I hoped I was wrong, but…

"Ladies and gentlemen, for those who don't know me, my name is Edward Palmer," he said. His expression and arrogant tone suggested he was the type of man who really loved to hear himself talk. "I'm so happy we're all here tonight to shower the couple of the hour with well wishes and congratulations on their surprise wedding this morning. Can we get a round of applause for Bernard Bentington and his new wife, Margo?"

He waved to the happy couple as the crowd erupted with applause. Bentington walked up the steps, his smiling wife trailing behind him. She looked radiant in a shimmering gold dress, topped off with diamonds in her ears and around her neck. The room felt alive as her jewels sparkled under the lights.

Wolf caught my eye as he maneuvered through the crowd, camera held high over his head. As Bentington spoke, thanking the crowd for their support, Wolf got to the front of the on lookers, taking picture after picture.

I knew what he was up to by getting so close, scanning Margo and looking for a hiding spot for her penny. Glancing around, Luna was well on her way to a Best Actress Award, talking up a storm to the ladies from the Rhino, all of whom were supposed to have a chance to wish upon the lucky coin.

Finishing up with a round of applause from the guests, the pair eventually left the stage and separated as they mingled about. Several of the women I'd seen at the Rhino and the hotel began to crowd around Margo. All wore smiles and dresses designed to catch the eye of every man in the room.

From the corner of my eye, I saw *her,* and my heart stopped.

Miss Eva, grinning from ear to ear, walked in from the elevators like a hungry lioness strolling into a herd of fat gazelles, none of whom knew the danger behind that primal smile. Like Luna, the mistress of the Golden Rhino wore red, only this color was tinted a few shades darker, making the woman look as if she'd been dipped in blood.

Four men wearing tuxes were on each side of her. While her eyes locked on to me, theirs looked about the room. Giving a gentle twist of her elbows, she shook her men off. Given their strong jawlines and athletic builds, I guessed they were the masculine side of the Rhino's staff. It wasn't clear if they were looking for men or women, but with a whisper from their boss, they left her side and disappeared into the crowd.

Half a dozen of her white-suited lackeys moved in behind her. From the looks, they were all Cuban, like Carlos. When she stopped, the men moved and flanked her, three to a side, forming a line with their boss in the center. Our eyes met, and I could imagine her hoping, praying for me to cross that line.

Picking up a champagne flute from a silver tray carried by one of the wait staff, I casually sipped the bubbly as I made my way towards her.

Ginger walked up behind Miss Eva, her face coated with makeup to cover her bruised cheek. As she walked, I noticed her green strapless number drew the attention of several men. When she saw me, her lips curled up in a mischievous grin. As she sidled up to her boss, Miss Eva looked over her face.

"Did Julie do your makeup?" Miss Eva asked sweetly.

Ginger nodded. "Yes, ma'am."

"That girl can do wonders." Eva must have noticed Ginger's side glances at me. "No, hun, get that out of your head right now. He isn't worth the effort. He has a girl, from what I understand, and judging from that suit, doesn't have money or taste. Besides..." She rubbed her right cheek, "He hits girls. Keep your head in the game and your eyes on their checkbooks."

Ginger frowned and started walking towards me.

Once clear of Miss Eva's line of sight, she gave me a wink and a sly smile. I responded with a tilt of the head before turning my attention back to Miss Eva.

"Fancy meeting you here." I couldn't help but smirk. "Here to make sure your girls and boys find a rich hubby, or maybe just entice some new names onto the club's membership roster?"

"If you weren't such a pain in my ass, Mr. Dietrich, I might spare you. But as it is, I wouldn't plan on seeing daybreak if I were you."

She looked me up and down as I waved over one of the wait staff. Snatching up another flute from his tray, I handed it to Miss Eva.

"Hitting a woman, Mr. Dietrich. Not very chivalrous, don't you think?" she said as the flute lifted to her mouth.

"Pointing a gun at a guest in your place. Not very friendly, wouldn't you say?"

"Touché, Mr. Dietrich. I'm curious about something. Have you actually got a plan? It seems like you're just flying by the seat of your pants."

"While I was in the marines, they drilled three words into our heads. Three little words that have made all the difference in my life. Improvise, adapt, and overcome." Feelings of my time in the Pacific drew out all the pleasantry in my expression.

"You'll be dead by daybreak." Her words came

out soft and sweet, as if I would enjoy my end.

"Likewise, my dear. I'm expecting a horde of demons to arrive. And so, you know, I deal with demons all the time, and trust me on this, they are not picky about who they kill. Friend or foe," I said and watched her face darken. "Of course, they may like red-heads. They say gingers don't have souls. Maybe they'll put that to the test with you."

"I know you prefer blondes, hun."

Her remark made my face twitch.

"The demon, I think you called him Barkley, came by again, after you and your friends left. He told me all about your sleeping girl as well as the other members of your motley crew. Spoke of their motivations for competing in his game of chance. Seems that Mr. Barkley is willing to pay handsomely for the coin's return and offered me a seat at the table to compete for the rewards. He seems rather concerned you three can't handle Mr. Barbas alone."

I downed the drink and did my best not to squeeze the flute hard enough to shatter it. Barkley was seriously pissing me off today.

I cleared my throat. "That so? Told you everything, did he? Does this mean you have a soul you're fighting for?"

"Immortality," she laughed. "He told you the Jameson story? Same kind of deal. An eternal legacy of sex, lust, and power, all stamped with my name forever."

Then a strange look appeared on her face as she stroked her abdomen. "And a daughter who'll inherit it all and keep my bloodline going."

Her hand trembled as she brought it to her face, rubbing her chin and cheek. Her eyes had a faraway look as she continued.

"I shook his hand, made the deal, then he took me... like no man ever has or ever will."

Her eyes moved to me, and she seemed to snap back to reality.

"Wait, he already..." I motioned to her stomach, and she nodded. "What if you lose?"

She scoffed. "Me? Lose? On the off chance that I do, Barkley takes the child. He said something about a workshop in Hell."

My mouth dropped open. How could she be so cold as the risk the life of a baby to an eternity of servitude in Hell. The image of Lily's face as a teenager popped into my thoughts. She'd been so perfect, so pure. And now...

"Who do I kill first? You and your companions?"

She raised her glass, sipping as she looked around the room. I could see her study of the room wasn't casual.

"Barbas," I said and watched her head tilt,

seeming to invite an explanation. "You and your boys aren't used to fighting demons. Wolf and I are. And it'll take all of us to stop them."

Unless Barbas has some serious backup, I thought Wolf and I could handle things, but she didn't need to know that. And, I didn't need her shooting us in the back while we dealt with the demons.

"When do you think they'll arrive?" she asked.

"Just tell your men to be ready," I explained. "When Barbas and his demons get here, they'll look…"

Miss Eva acted uninterested. "We've seen him and some of his crew. We'll know'em if we see'em."

She downed the last of her champagne and held out the empty glass to me. "Be a lamb and do something with that."

When I didn't take it, she glared through narrowed eyes. "What do you want, Mr. Dietrich?"

I couldn't help but snort at the question and took her flute.

"What do I want? I want a lot of things. I want the vacation I promised my girlfriend. I want a world where demons and monsters occasionally take a fucking day off so that I can too. I want people like you to pay for your sins. Instead, all I have is a sharp stick, a pair of well used fists, a headache the size of Wyoming, and a serious lack of coffee."

She smiled. "Just not been a good day for you, has it? Well, if it's a comfort, there is an open bar. Just take it easy on the drink. Since I'm being generous and letting you live for a while longer, I need you at your best when the demons arrive."

With that, she strolled off with Carlos, who moved up to her side while keeping a respectful distance. The man glared at me through a pair of blackened eyes. I glanced around as her men slowly positioned themselves throughout the room. Like it or not, the goons knew what they were doing, making sure they had all sides of the room covered or within their firing arc.

Scanning the room again, I found Margo, still at the center of a flock of women. Both Luna and Miss Eva were slowly weaving their way through the crowd, towards her. A bald man stood close to the center of the crowd. He'd been on the stage with the newlyweds, standing in the background.

A bodyguard? I wondered and studied him.

When an opening appeared briefly between us, I spotted the telltale bulge of a pistol holstered under his left arm.

Wolf appeared at my side, holding the camera and taking a quick photo. "Enjoying the party, sir? I see our girl has a bodyguard. I wonder if it was her idea or Bentington's?"

I nodded. "I don't know, but that's a good thing, I think. She'll need protection if shit goes down. Someone between the penny and the demons or Miss Eva's goons or both. Otherwise, he's just another obstacle for us, later on down the road."

Luna's blonde locks danced as she moved, reminding me of Natalie. My thoughts dwelled on her for a moment, wondering what she'd think of a party like this. Clearing my throat, I called for another drink, trading the two empty flutes for a full one.

"How many of those have you had?" Wolf asked.

"I do my best work when I'm not entirely sober," I responded.

As I took the first sip, a man caught my attention. Far in the back of the room, he towered over the others, at least a foot taller than the closest individual. Chiseled features and the build of a professional linebacker set him apart from everyone else. His black eyes swiveled in my direction and narrowed. For a brief moment, I swore I saw flames within them.

"Barbas," Wolf said.

His hand, the size of a Christmas ham, waved over the crowd, pointing in my direction. Other white-suited men, hidden by his bulk and the party's attendees, emerged from the sea of humanity. In a slow and deliberate fashion, they started fanning out through the room, maneuvering to surround me. They too were large and impressive. All were blond and bearded, and all had those same dark eyes. The image of the Norse god of thunder came to my mind.

Oh goodie, a flock of Thors.

Without thinking, my hands slipped into my jacket, pulling out the twin .45 caliber Colt automatics. The crowd, already picking up on the tension in the air, became restless. The metallic sound of a Tommy gun's bolt being pulled back and released rang out. Glancing back, I saw Carlos and his men readying their weapons. I only hoped that when the lead started flying, they remembered to shoot the demons and not everyone else.

Barbas's attention had shifted from me to Wolf. The anger in his expression made it clear those two had unresolved issues from the fight Wolf had described earlier. Looking to the group of women surrounding Margo, I saw they were quickly dispersing, while Miss Eva and Luna both still tried to fight their way to grab the newlywed first.

"Margo Bentington! Bring her to me! I command it!" Barbas shouted.

Sixteen

Barbas's voice thundered, so loud everyone threw hands up to cover their ears. People screamed, and some windows shattered under the force of the sound. I could actually feel my ribs rattle under the impact of the noise.

"Oh, to hell with you," Wolf yelled, and charged the imposing demon, only to be tackled mid-stride by two others.

I raised my pistols but pulled my fingers off the triggers when the crowd panicked, obscuring my view. I managed to push my way through for a short distance before I felt a hand wrap around my upper arm. Turning, I saw one of the demons, smiling. As he jerked me around, smacking several bystanders in the process, I pushed the barrel of a gun again his neck and fired.

He hurled me into the crowd and sent me sliding on my back. Jumping to my feet, I ran through the wave of fleeing people, back towards him. Slumped over, he had his hands on his neck. On Earth and in human form, demons are vulnerable to wounds and death like a human. Albeit it, their bodies can take a hell of a lot of punishment first. But if they died on Earth, they'd return to Hell and await their next chance to be summoned up by some stupid cultist or by a greater demon.

Stunned and hurting, he must not have expected me to be firing silver bullets. They were meant to kill vampires and werewolves, but the blessed drop of water captured inside the silver would burn a demon like acid.

I got behind him. It meant taking a chance, but I slammed a foot into his upper right calf, forcing the knee to give and his leg to buckle. Writhing and howling, he dropped to a kneeling position. Shoving both barrels against the base of his skull, I pulled the triggers, firing upwards into his head. Scarlet blood and brains painted the floor in front of him. He remained upright for a few seconds before toppling over, prone and unmoving.

"That felt too easy," I muttered.

No sooner than I'd spoken the words did hands

grab me. The lack of anything beneath my feet didn't register until I'd hit the floor and slid again. Like a bowling ball, my body slammed into leg after leg, sending running bystanders to the floor like pins.

I finally stopped, sat upright, and shook my head to stop my spinning thoughts and vision. Looking up, I had just enough time to see the demon who'd thrown me pull his fist back. His fist slammed into my face like a wrecking ball.

The world lost all sound except for a loud whine. Everything flashed white as the blow sent me down, smacking the back of my head against the floorboards. Making myself focus, I could still feel the handle of one of the Colts in my left hand.

I fired twice into the demon's chest at near point-blank range. He jerked from each impact but kicked at me in the ribs. From the pain, I couldn't be sure he hadn't broken one. Seeing his foot pull back again, I rolled. The kick missed, but I felt the wind from it breeze by me. I twisted upwards, shoving my barrel into his groin, and fired.

Blood sprayed out, and he jumped back, grabbing his crotch. I aimed as well as I could at his forehead. The bullet flew high, so I fired another. This one hit, blowing out the back of his skull and ending him for the night.

I fell back onto the floor and assessed my

condition. Taking a deep breath, fire erupted in my chest. I touched the spot on my ribcage where the demon had kicked me.

"These guys are too easy. Must be the second-string players." I muttered and wondered where the big bads were hiding.

A third demon screamed with rage, garnering my attention. His footfalls shook the floor as he charged me from across the room. By this time, most of the guests had either cleared out or taken shelter behind the bar. He wasn't as tall as Barbas, but he made up for it in bulk. Dark claws jutted out of his fingertips, like a switchblade.

"Well, shit."

Scrambling to my feet, I saw my other pistol, lying nearby. Grabbing it, I twisted back towards him, hissing as pain shot through me. Leveling both weapons at the charging demon, I hesitated. Too many civilians cowered along the far wall, behind the running demon. Any bullet I fired could injure any one of them. I swore to myself. It wasn't a chance I could afford to take.

I had just enough time to holster my pistols and draw my trusty wooden stake. Though it was meant for vampires, this gift from a holy man could wreak havoc on a demon. At least, I sure as hell hoped it would.

I leapt to the side, and the demon's charging swing missed, but he stopped and turned faster than I thought he could. A couple of his claws sliced through my jacket's sleeve and shirt, opening a deep gash on my left bicep.

Grunting, I spun and jabbed the stake into the demon's thigh before ripping it back out. Dodging and ducking as he repeatedly swung his claws, I jockeyed for a position to go for his chest. We painted the floor with each other's blood as we danced back and forth, each of us connecting here and there. His claws slicing into my upper back and shoulders, my wood tearing gashes in his right arm and torso.

The demon lunged, trying to catch me in his arms. Dropping almost to the floor, I spun and kicked at his feet. My shoe connected and hooked around his ankle, and I jerked my leg back.

The demon roared as he fell. I threw my arm out, twisting the stake so that it stood like a soldier at attention beneath the demon. The scream tore through my skull as he jerked oddly before rising to his knees. He grabbed my right ankle as he got to his feet and lifted me so quick I saw blurs around me. Wind rushed by my face, and I realized I was flying through the air.

My body collided with something that gave way on impact. When I heard the shattering of glass, I knew the window had slowed my flight, but I was still going. Whipping my arms out, I grabbed the windowsill. Searing pain ripped through my hand, and I couldn't help but let go. My other hand seized the brick ledge as I began to fall again.

Agony stabbed all along my hands and arms, but I held tight. I'd sliced my fingers to the bone on my left hand. I hung there for a moment. Pulling myself upwards and digging my shoes into the brickwork, I managed to loop an arm over the windowsill, avoiding the remaining glass shards. It took a few minutes of work, before I was able to re-enter the party.

The demon who'd thrown me, staggered around with my stake in his abdomen. Glancing to my left, Wolf busied himself by slugging it out with a pair of demons. Barbas stood to the side, smiling as he watched Wolf's struggle. When his eyes focused on me, he barked a command in some unknown language and pointed to me.

The blade-fingered demon looked in my direction. Grabbing my stake, I thought he might pull it out. When his fingers wrapped around the handle, though, he screamed, and smoke boiled up from between his digits. His flesh had come into contact with the holy symbols etched into it. Staggering back and letting go, he looked back to me. He flexed his arms, roared, and charged at me again.

Tired, bleeding, and in a lot of pain, all I could think to do was to pull out a small bottle of holy water from my jacket pocket. I planned to throw it on him when he got close enough. Problem was, by the time I had it in my hands, he was on me.

His thick, sweaty hands grabbed me, lifting me off the ground by the collar. His claws tore through more fabric and opened deep gouges in my chest and right shoulder. My knee grazed the stake jutting from his midsection like a thorn. Glaring into his eyes, I reared back and threw my knee forward, driving the stake deeper into his gut.

The demon grunted and dropped me, staggering back. The moment my feet hit the ground, I dropped to a squat and kicked out again, tripping him up and sending him to floor. The demon landed on his back, arms thrown wide.

I jumped onto him, yanking the stake free with one hand and shoving the bottle of holy water into the two-inch wide wound. Twisting the cork as I pulled my hand out, I made sure the divine fluid would flow out into the demonic creature.

The effect was instantaneous. The demon began to howl, thrashing and grabbing at the wound. But it was lodged too deep inside, and the damage was already done. Death, although temporary, would come for him soon.

The holy water dissolved his flesh like acid and got into the demon's bloodstream. He threw me off as he writhed, sending me to the floor where my skull hit the wood planks again.

Standing and staggering back, I watched as the giant demon began to fall apart. As is typical with dead or dying demons, what flesh remained broke down into its base elements, turning to a sickening green mist and flowing away like an ill fog.

Flexing my fingers around the stake felt like holding them to an electric hotplate, but I pushed the pain away. I snapped my eyes to Barbas. He stared daggers at me. The feeling was mutual.

Wolf was still fighting his two demons and the big man was holding his own. One looked ready to drop and the other seemed full of piss and vinegar.

I'd ignored the occasional gunshots after the first appearance of the demons, but now so much lead was being thrown into the air that I looked around at the rest of the room. Miss Eva's goons had opened up on another pair of demons that were chasing Margo, her elderly husband, and his entourage.

A crowd of people banged on the elevator doors, waiting for them to reopen. The smart ones had already clogged the stairwells. Screams and violence filled the night.

I started to run in towards the elevator but threw myself to the floor as the Tommy guns opened up. The goons weren't aiming, just spraying towards the demons.

Bullets, scores of them, flew over my head. I saw at least a dozen people, panicked and caught in the crossfire, fall. Drawing *Miss J*, my favorite pistol, I took careful aim and fired into the back of one of the demons.

The bullet struck, but I don't think the demon realized from where the shot had come. The goon's bullets were having little effect, but my silver one got some attention. Instead of pursuing Margo, the demons turned and attacked Miss Eva's men, sparing the innocents. Within seconds, white-suited bodies, mostly intact, were flying around the room.

A bell dinged. Every head turned as doors on both elevators opened. In a mad rush, people flooded into them. I saw blonde hair and, as she turned, Margo looked right at me with eyes wide with fear. We locked eyes briefly until the doors closed.

In the other elevator, the rich fought the rich as panicked guests battled for space. Carlos held out an arm, blocking others and paving the way for a pair of redheads, Miss Eva and Ginger. When the doors refused to close because of overcrowding, Miss Eva nodded, and Carlos shoved Ginger back into the room and into harm's way.

Looking back to Barbas, I raised a hand and gestured with my finger, inviting him to dance. He snarled in anger as I smiled in delight. His demons had their chance to stop me, now it was our turn to dance.

He came at me fast. No civilians cowered or hid behind him, so I dropped the stake to the floor and drew the Colts. I loosed a hailstorm of silver at him. My index fingers rapidly worked the well-oiled triggers, empting the magazines. Blurring, he dodged from side to side. Most of the shots missed. Knowing I'd never have time to reload, I dropped the pistols and grabbed the stake again.

Barbas careened into me before I could dodge or ready the stake. As I flew back, a large hand grabbed me by the arm and pulled me to him. With the stake being held in the hand that Barbas held, the weapon was useless. With my free hand, I reached around to my belt and pulled a silver push dagger from its sheath. Wrapping my sliced, bleeding fingers around the handle felt like grabbing a live electrical line, but I fought through the pain and attacked. I slammed the blade deep into his forearm. Its razor-sharp blade penetrated one side, and the slender tip emerged from the other.

The massive demon shrieked while I grunted and

swore as the handle pushed against the open wounds in my fingers. Barbas's eyes bore into me. Anger, flickering like feverish flames from the hottest lakes in Hell, burned in his expression.

He dropped me and grabbed the push dagger, drawing it out in a fast, fluid movement. When my feet hit the floor, I staggered and almost fell, but somehow managed to stay upright. The momentary distraction gave him the opportunity to step back.

The clank of metal on the floor echoed through the room as he dropped my push dagger. The sleeve of his white jacket glistened as scarlet blood flowed from the wound, dripping down over his hands and splattering on the wood planks.

Pissed, hurting, and just flat-out wanting this to end, one way or another, I held up my finger and invited him to make his best move. He grinned and, in a puff is wind, disappeared only to reappear directly behind me.

I knew the trick and ducked as his fist zoomed by me. Spinning, I thrust the stake at him. He deflected the strike, knocking me off balance and then backhanded me across the room.

I found myself on my back, every nerve ending swearing at me. My hands were empty beside me. God only knew where my weapons lay, scattered across the room most likely. I needed time to think of a way out of this.

"You're going to lose, you know." I stared into his black eyes and swallowed hard.

Blood dribbled from my split lip and bleeding nose. The metallic taste of blood filled my mouth, and my face throbbed.

"There are too many of us. You can fight me all night. You might even kill me, but the others will get the penny and they'll get it to Barkley. I'd say you need a bigger army, but your demons are too stupid for the subtlety that's required for a job like this."

At the mention of Barkley's name, Barbas' eyes widened. That was a bit of a surprise. Surely, he had to have known the other demon was in on the hunt for the penny. Then again, why would he have known? Could I use it to my advantage?

Coughing, I spit some blood onto the floor at his feet and then looked up into his dark eyes. "Margo has done well hiding it from you, hasn't she? Did you feel it here tonight?"

Barbas slammed his foot into my chest. I took the damage in stride and smiled up at him. He kicked me again, this hit impacting the same spot his underling had.

"Frustrating, isn't it? Outsmarted by a mere human. And this must be the really infuriating part for you, she's getting everything she wants. Foiled by your own lucky creation. And here I am. Only a man, flesh and blood, and yet I discovered what she's using to hide it from you. Barkley said you'd had to eat crow when you lost the bet with Jameson a century ago. And now he's gonna get the penny and you'll have to face Lucifer and explain how you failed, again."

His eyes darted around the room, hesitating, just as I hoped he would. He turned briefly to look at the last of his demons. Before falling, Miss Eva's boys had cut down another with enough lead that there was nothing left of him but goo. The last remaining demon on the other side of the room was busy shredding the last of the goons. With all their bullets fired, they stood little chance of surviving.

A quick look at Wolf filled my heart with hope. He'd taken down one demon and had the other on its back. Wolf pounded his fists into the struggling creature's bloody face, a blast of holy light flashing from the rings on each impact.

"Your turn to lose, but you're just a man. Men like you are a dime a dozen," Barbas said.

He grabbed my jacket with one hand, curling the material up between his thick fingers, and lifted me from the floor. I spotted the stake laying a few feet away from where I'd been. Too far for me to reach, but maybe…

My left hand fumbled through my jacket pocket for the second bottle of holy water. The blood seeping from my fingers acted like grease on the glass. Every time I wrapped my fingers around it, the bottle would slip out.

I had to think fast.

"A man! Just a man? You don't know who I am, do you?" I hissed.

"You're human." Barbas sneered, growing louder with each word. "A disease the Father cursed upon this earth and upon my kind. We were the rightful ones. We should have been given this world, to shape into an angelic paradise. Instead, he created you... gave you all the glory and kept us in our heavenly slave roles. We were pure! You're nothing but corruptible organic shit. A pestilence that devours and gives nothing in return."

"To hell with you, Barbas. Do your worst. I've fought bigger and meaner things than you. Why do you think Barkley wanted me in this damn coin hunt to begin with? Because he and Lucifer know I'm not one to be trifled with." I smirked.

His smile widened. "And who are you then, little human?"

Something started happening, something I'd not experienced before. I felt heat on my face, neck, and chest. The smell of scorching cloth filled my nostrils, and smoke filled my eyes. Looking down at his hand, I saw that his skin was glowing from within. Smoke rose, and small flames licked out from between his fingers where he held me up by the jacket. My shirt and jacket were about to burst into flames.

Twisting my head, I returned his smile and ignored the smoke. My left hand finally seized the bottle in my pocket and popped the top.

"I'm Thomas Fucking Dietrich. Scourge of demons and devils. Killer of the behemoth of Kwenta Island."

His expression changed at the mention of Kwenta. He may never have seen me but knew who I was and what I'd done. Even in Hell, scary stories are told about that damned island.

I leaned forward, getting as close to his face as possible. "And I am your worst fucking nightmare."

Before he could react, I dumped the holy water onto his face. It instantly began melting his flesh. He released me and desperately wiped the burning fluid from his eyes. I hit the ground and dove to the left to avoid his thrashing arms. I tucked and rolled, coming up on my feet, grabbing my stake in the process.

I patted my chest to put out a couple of smoldering spots on my collar and charged. I hoped to get the stake into his chest, but he turned to look at me, and I swerved and slid a few feet away. One eye had melted away, but the other focused on me, fury burning within it.

He took a step towards me. "Behemoth killer? You die now. The coin is nothing compared to the glory I'll receive, escorting your soul to Hell."

"I think you've done enough," a woman's voice called out a split second before a bottle exploded against the side of Barbas' head.

I looked at Ginger, who stood to the right and behind the demon.

She winked at me. "I got this handsome. I've dealt with bigger brutes before."

Ginger held a lit cigarette lighter in her hands, which she promptly tossed at him. As it soared towards him, Barbas turned the full fury of his hatred towards her. Bulls-eye! The lighter smacked against Barbas' skull, and the fluid splashed across him ignited in a flash of yellow and blue flames. The heat from the ignition warmed my skin and brought a smile to my face.

Barbas screamed, tearing off his burning jacket and shirt. The flames died out quickly, leaving his head and torso burnt, yet the demon still lived. Standing too close, Ginger didn't get a chance to run as he spun, rushed her, and grabbed her by the neck. Effortlessly, he lifted the young woman off her feet.

I thought I had an opening with his attention on

Ginger and charged, but Barbas turned. He swung his free hand and caught me by surprise. The force of the blow sent me backwards, slamming me hard into the wall below a windowsill. The impact knocked the wind from my lungs. Each attempt to take a breath felt like daggers being shoved between every rib.

"Let me show you how to use fire, little girl." Barbas' laugh echoed throughout the room.

With one hand around Ginger's neck, he placed his other hand on top of her skull. As they had with me and my jacket, his hands began to glow. She struggled to scream through the chokehold.

I rolled, trying to get up, but the lack of air made me dizzy. My guns were on the floor, out of reach. All I could do was watch.

Smoke, followed by sparks, erupted from between his fingers. The putrid stench of burning hair flooded the room as Ginger's beautiful red mane turned to flames. She struggled, thrashing her arms, but to no avail. Her pale skin reddened, then blackened before the flesh around her skull burst into flames.

"No!" I tried to scream over and over.

I know she was still alive, for the first few seconds anyway. Her flaming lips moved, screaming without making a sound. Her eyelid squeezed open and shut.

And then it was over. He let her go, and Ginger's

body dropped to the floor, landing in a smoking heap.

A tear rolled down my cheek. She didn't deserve it. She wouldn't die in vain. The bastard would die, one way or another.

I could still see her on fire in my mind, could still hear her silent screaming. Choking down my guilt and anger, I forced myself to take slow, steady gulps of air, shallow at first. I ignored the footfalls and shouts as I worked to get my body working again.

"You deserve a better death. It'll be painful one, long and agonizing, and before it ends, you'll beg for something as quick as that bitch's demise." Barbas' voice was close now.

I opened my eyes and saw him mere feet from me. The pain in my chest had subsided, and my breathing had steadied.

Behind him, movement caught my attention. The putrid smoke from Ginger lingered behind him, but suddenly shifted. An image could almost be made out, as if someone were walking through it.

Atta girl, Luna, I thought.

"He may be a dick, but he's my friend. And no one hurts my friends," Luna shouted.

Brilliant flashes of fire strobed in unison with the sound of a gunshot. Although I couldn't see the gun, I couldn't contain the smile as Luna opened up on the demon with a Tommy gun. She screamed in anger or fury, but kept the trigger pulled back.

Barbas grunted with each impact, hunching over as the stream of flaming hot lead poured into him. After the last round fired, freed from the onslaught, he struck out, backhanding the invisible Luna. She hit the floor, turning visible as she slid to a stop, some thirty feet away.

I took advantage of the moment and hurled myself at Barbas, slamming into him and ramming the stake into his back, near where his heart should be. Wrapping my free arm around his neck I placed my other palm on the butt of the stake and pushed it in further.

Barbas screamed and grabbed me, whipping me around. Hanging by my arm in front of him, I intentionally didn't move my eyes when I saw movement behind him again. Instead I looked the demon in the eye and laughed.

"Tell your boss who beat you and sent you back to that shithole you call home," I snarled.

Wolf, having dispatched his last demon, raced across the room, slamming his fist into the butt of the stake. I both heard and saw the point emerge through the demon's chest.

Again, Barbas dropped me. He loomed over me, unmoving and letting a low growl slowly wheeze out as his lungs emptied. Without a word, his body began to melt away. Rivulets of green smoke poured from him and spread across the floor as he dissolved before our eyes. By the end, nothing was left except my stake, which lay where his feet had once stood.

"Is he gone?" Luna asked.

I turned as she approached. "Yes. Gone. Thanks for the distraction."

Turning, I looked where the Cubans had been fighting. They were gone and so was the last demon.

Luna watched as the last of the green mist floated away. Her breath quickened, and the blood drained from her face. Wolf stepped to her side and held her before she dropped.

"It's okay, hun. You did good," he whispered, and kissed her cheek.

"You okay?" I asked.

She nodded. "I—I can't believe I did that. I hate guns, but God, what a rush."

"You took a hard hit. Everything feel in order?" I asked.

She looked up at me through narrowed eyes. "You two took more hits than I did. Besides, I can take a punch. After all, I grew up in Chicago."

Looking around, I exhaled. "Margo get out okay? I saw them in the elevators."

"Yes. Bentington's men got her and the old man out. They said they were taking the newlyweds back to the manor," Luna said, her voice regaining its usual composure. "I ran some interference with Miss Eva. Blocked her and her right-hand man from getting into the elevators with Margo."

"Miss Eva know where they're going?" Wolf asked.

Luna laughed. "Maybe not. I yelled a couple of times into her goon's ear that Bentington's plane was ready for their honeymoon, that they were going straight to the airport."

She laughed again. "I even cracked a joke about it. What a way to start their honeymoon."

"Nice plan," I said, grinning.

"What now?" Luna asked.

'My guess is that they're heading home," Wolf said.

Checking my watch, I frowned. "I agree. We need to get to my car and get to Bentington's place. There's only four hours till midnight."

Luna nuzzled against Wolf, while I collected my dropped weapons, reloading the pistols and holstering them. My gaze briefly landed on Ginger, and my heart sank.

Stepping to an over-turned table, I picked up several roses that had once been part of a centerpiece. I moved to stoop down beside the fallen woman.

Swallowing hard, I forced myself to look at her.

In our brief war with the demons, Ginger revealed her true character, brave and self-sacrificing. I laid the roses on her and bowed my head.

"I'm so sorry. You didn't deserve this. My life wasn't worth losing yours, but I'll always be grateful for…" I paused, not sure what else I could say to honor the fallen woman.

Wolf and Luna stood, glancing between Ginger and me but not saying a word. I rose up, turning to look at them. I saw the look in Luna's eyes. It matched the one in Wolf's and my own, an overwhelming determination to win.

"Time to end this."

Seventeen

I wasn't certain of our destination as I pulled my Studebaker out of the parking garage, but I felt much better being on the move. I knew the area where the Bentington Estate sat; I just wasn't sure about the exact street or street number. Handing the city map and flashlight to Luna, who sat in the rear seat with Wolf, I asked for directions. She'd been there before, and so shouldn't have a problem finding it.

The Windyke-Southwind neighborhood was hell and gone from downtown. Full of huge manor homes and a gated country club, it was the home to many of the city's elite families.

"Got a plan?" Wolf asked and eyed the woman on his left.

"Not yet. Thinking," I replied, uncertain of what

we'd do when we got there.

A few blocks into our drive, I heard a slap. Glancing back, Wolf held up his hand, shaking the pain away.

"Did you slap him?" I jokingly asked Luna.

"He keeps trying to help me with the map," Luna said, never looking away from the unfolded paper.

I could see the confusion on his face and the serious one on hers.

"With the way you've been flirting with me all day, I figured you'd like help," Wolf said.

Again, Luna answered without looking away from the map. "Hun, I wasn't busy earlier. When I'm bored, I'm flirty. Right now, I need to concentrate and guide Mister Monster Killer to the right place. Speaking of which, make the next right then the second left you come to."

"Luna is it just black men or Wolf in particular that gets you fired up?" The question was meant to be playful, but I saw her expression darken from light-hearted to melancholy.

"It's a long story and an old one," she whispered, and leaned against the door.

"Hey, I'm not mad about the flirting. It's just that I'm engaged to someone else." Wolf leaned over to her and whispered something the road noise drowned out.

"We've got a while. I'd like to hear the story," I said, glancing back.

"No better way to deal with an old memory that haunts you than to share it with others," Wolf said.

True," I said, and then laughed. "I'd tell you some of mine, but it sounds like the best one was in that damn book you two already read."

She shifted uncomfortably but gave into our unrelenting words of encouragement to tell the story.

"Ten years ago, I'd just turned sixteen and started liking boys. There was a black boy that'd I'd always been friends with. We lived in one of those poor areas of Chicago where no cared what color your neighbors were. His name was Robby, and we grew close."

She shifted in her seat again. "One day, we snuck into an alley, found a secluded spot, and he kissed me. It didn't stop with one. Thing is, we didn't realize that some older boys, white boys, were on the fire escape watching us. They dropped down, beat the hell out of Robby, and dragged him out of the alley. Tossed him in the back of a pick-up truck and took off."

She wiped a tear from her cheek.

"What happened then?" Wolf asked.

Her voice cracked as she spoke. "I screamed for help. Fought and tried to pull him free. Finally, one of the guys punched me, calling me a whore and a coon-lover. They got in the truck and tore out of there, leaving me on the ground with all the neighbors staring, but none willing to help."

Wolf moaned and turned to look out the window. I shared his sentiment.

"They found him a few days later, in some woods near Jolliet, swinging from a tree." Another tear fell and was wiped away.

"I'm so sorry, hun." I felt bad for pushing her to tell us the story.

She looked at Wolf and smiled. "When I picture him in my mind, you know, older. Well, you look like the kind of man I think he'd have become. Big, strapping, but with gentle eyes and a big heart."

Wolf leaned back in his seat and stared at the floor. "I, um… I'm honored you think that."

"After that, I turned to crime." Her tone changed from sad to defiant. "I wanted out of the neighborhood, out of that life. I wanted revenge."

"You're not a witch or, what did you call yourself? You specialize in only a few spells, all of which are geared to help you with your thieving work. I've been around too long to know that real witches, no matter how practiced or experienced, need a circle to cast or components to offer up," I said. She nodded.

"Every witch I've seen is willing to cast any kind

of spell. If you could do that, you could already have had this case wrapped up," Wolf added.

"My mother was a witch and started teaching me things from the time I stepped out of diapers. My favorite was an invisibility spell. I loved casting and sneaking about. Drove mom crazy, but she appreciated my skills. When I was ten, she and I talked about my magical future. I told her I wanted to specialize. I wanted to be an Illusionist."

"What does that mean?" Wolf asked.

"It means that I don't need elaborate spell ceremonies or the stars to be in alignment to do what I want. Most magic has a religious nature, drawing on the light or the dark energies. But not all spells need the divine or the devil to work. I have a small number of spells that draw on the power of nature instead. Took me years to get them right, but I can cast them fast and easy," she explained.

"Must be handy. What all can you do?" I asked and turned the wheel as we rounded another corner.

"Make myself invisible, silent, and with concentration and a little luck, create minor illusions, but that's all. No big spell book in my closet."

Luna stopped and looked at the map. "Go through the light and take the first left."

"With tricks like that, I guess you've amassed a fortune," Wolf joked.

She sighed. "I knew enough back when Robby was beaten that I could have done something. I was just too scared. Stupid, stupid. After that, I started stealing. Money, food, whatever. I wanted to get my mom and me out of there, out of that place. And we did move into a nice place a few months later, but I've never really forgiven myself."

Silence filled the car for a while as the city streets fell behind us and we entered the suburbs.

"And the revenge part?" Wolf asked.

She looked at him, her jaw quivering. "I… I planted stolen stuff in their homes, their cars, in their pockets and told the police. Planted drugs and whatever I could until the police locked them away for decades." She laughed. "When the police heard they'd killed a black boy, it wasn't any big deal. But tell them three boys stole some watches from a white-owned jewelry store, and they came down on the guys like the hammer of God."

Wolf nodded and whispered, "True."

Luna cleared her throat and spoke up. Her tone was flat and to the point.

"Guys. When we get the penny, I don't want it. I made the deal with Barkley for help with my mother. A couple of years ago, she turned over some evidence that put away one of Chicago's leading gangsters. Thing is, they don't know it was her. Rumor is that the mobster, a guy named Blant, has his lieutenants combing the town for the snitch. The cops did a good job of keeping her identity a secret. They may never know it was her but that doesn't stop me from worrying. Barkley offered me a deal. He could doctor the files so that if the gangsters ever got someone on the inside of the department, they couldn't find out it was my mom who squealed."

"What was your mother doing with the gang?" Wolf asked.

"She's gifted at telling fortunes. It's the kinda thing that comes in handy at the track, if you know what I mean," Luna said, then paused before continuing.

"You know, I have gifts that others would kill for, and all I've done is use them for selfish reasons. Watching the way you two fought tonight... well, it makes me want to do something better. Like, maybe... become a P.I."

I glanced over my shoulder at her. "I think you'd make a damn good one."

"Me too," Wolf added.

"One of you deserve the penny, more than me. I'll help out, of course," she said.

Wolf shook his head. "Same here. Dietrich, I saw your girl. She got duped by Barkley. You're not doing this for yourself, you're doing it for love. Me?

I'm getting paid by a rich client to get the penny and save a rich, spoiled boy. Hell, the kid doesn't even care if I succeed or not."

"Thomas, take the penny. Save your girl." Luna reached forward and put a hand on my shoulder and gave it a reassuring squeeze.

"Let's not jump to anything yet. The night's not over."

Eighteen

"We just going straight up the drive way?" Wolf asked.

I glanced back to Wolf and nodded. "Might as well. We don't have time for subtlety. Luna, go invisible and get upstairs to Margo's room. I know where she hides the penny."

She gave me a questioning look, so I added. "Where better to keep an unholy yet lucky coin? Her Bible. Even a cheap Bible is still the blessed Word of God."

"Got it," Luna replied, a grin spreading across her face.

"Wolf, you and I are going straight through the front door." I spun the steering wheel, dropped down a gear, and started up the long driveway.

"They'll have guards, considering the attack at the party," Wolf said, cracking his knuckles.

"I imagine they will. Look, we can't go in there, guns blazing. Everyone here should be human and we don't need that kind of trouble," I replied.

The manor house stood like a castle, lit by the silver glow of the moon. Only a handful of electric lights were on, casting an amber glow upon the front entranceway. Darkness engulfed the rest of the place. A lone car sat, parked at an odd angle compared to the door, indicating that it'd been parked in a hurry.

"Are you sure they came back here?" I asked.

Luna leaned forward, resting her arms on the seat and tilting her head to get a better view of the house as we closed in on it.

"There, the window by the door. I just saw someone looking out." She pointed.

I nodded. "Me too. I think they saw us and stepped back."

I slowed the car to a snail's pace as I glanced back. I saw Wolf but not Luna but felt the woman's breath on my neck.

"I'm gonna run around back, go in through the backdoor, and head straight up to the bedroom," she whispered. "I bet that's where it is. Good luck."

Pulling to a stop, we opened the car doors and stepped out. Looking around, I didn't see any trace of

Luna. I expected to at least hear her footfalls but heard only crickets. I was glad she didn't live in my town. I had enough to do with all the vampires, werewolves, and other unholy crap.

"Let's hold back for a few minutes, give her a little time to get inside," I said, pulling my pistols out.

I quickly checked the magazines in both pistols. Wolf did the same with his weapons. Glancing over to him, I had to admit that it felt nice to have a partner of sorts, for a change. This man held his own against a pair of demons and was ready for more. I liked that.

The thought brought Natalie to mind. She may not be able to punch a demon to death, but she had proven herself a good shot and a smarter companion. I missed having her at my side. She challenged me in ways I didn't realize I liked, until tonight. After this evening, I'd never take her presence for granted.

"Is it me, or was this supposed to be more of a challenge?" Wolf whispered.

"At least Miss Eva and her boys aren't here." I smiled, thinking about Luna's word play that sent them to the airport.

The flashes and reports of gunshots assaulted our senses. Without a word, we broke into a run. The front doors were unlocked. Stairs were ahead of me and rooms on either side. Movement to my right caught my attention, and I turned, ran, and stopped in the doorway to a spacious living room.

Three bodies lay on the floor, their blood splashed across the beige carpet. Margo stood on the far side of the room, looking at Wolf and me with a shit-eating grin. Her slender form was still wrapped in the evening gown from earlier, and her hands held a matching, sequined-covered clutch.

"Drop the weapons, now. Don't try to be heroes." The man's voice came from behind us.

Shaking my head, I bent and dropped my Colts to the carpet. Wolf followed suit, and we both looked back to see the bald man from the party, Margo's bodyguard, holding a large revolver. He narrowed his eyes at us, and his stance told me he was a professional.

"Into the living room. Careful not to step in the blood." He motioned with the gun, and we obeyed.

On a small table, beside the doorway to the living room, sat a telephone. I elbowed Wolf in the ribs.

"Give me some room, you overgrown bastard," I growled.

Wolf looked at me, tilting his head as I gave a subtle wink, and he shoved me hard to the side. Letting myself be carried by his act, I made myself trip up on my own feet and slammed into the table. Hoping no one noticed, I knocked the receiver off. Pushing myself up and forward, I blocked the phone from their view and coughing to cover the sound of the dial, I turned it and let it spin back to position. Listening hard, I heard the faint voice of an operator speaking on the line.

Straightening up, I rejoined Wolf and we entered the living room together.

"Mrs. Bentington, I'd like to say it's a pleasure, but considering your man has a gun pointed at me…" I let my words trail off. They weren't meant for her anyway.

I nodded at the bodies. "Actually, should I call you Mrs. Bentington or do you prefer Margo?"

Studying the bodies, I recognized Margo's new husband. Another wore a black suit, and I guessed he was the house butler. The last looked a lot like the driver I'd seen earlier, outside the law firm.

"You have perfect timing," Margo laughed.

"On your knees. Both of you," the guard said.

With some reluctance, we dropped to our knees. Pain shot though my joints in the process. Being thrown around like a rag-doll will do that. Assuming I lived through this, I knew I'd feel the night's effects for the next few weeks.

"Want to tell me why?" I said to Margo.

"Why kill my new husband? I wasn't planning on doing it so soon. I figured two or three months at the least, assuming he didn't wear his heart out in the bedroom. But then Miss Eva and those others showed up at the party, along with you two."

Looking over my shoulder to the guard, I smiled and winked. "Let me guess, she promised you a big wad of cash for killing everyone here."

"Or was it some quality time with her kitty?" Wolf quipped.

"Want me to kill them now?" The guard stepped around us, moving close to her and adjusting his grip on the weapon.

His gun remained trained on us. I didn't know if he was involved in this for money or for new-found love. I had to keep them to talking.

"Surely you know that…" I started but she cut me off.

"What? That the police will figure it all out? No. I don't think so," she said, and then tilted her head as the sounds of distant sirens just became audible.

"As soon as we got home, my late hubby insisted we call the police. The fool thought Miss Eva and her goons were behind everything and would follow us home. I knew she or you would show up here tonight," She stepped closer to the guard. "Oh yes, Ginger told me all about your visit and that you were looking for something. I knew it had to be the penny."

"She's dead, you know. Ginger. The big bad demon got her." I said and watched as her eyes widen.

Margo froze, her face betraying her shock. When she spoke, Margo tried to show she was in charge, but her uncertainty came through.

"That's unfortunate. She was a good girl. Is the demon dead?"

I nodded.

She craned her neck to get close to the bodyguard's ear. "Let me have the gun. I'll cover them while you call the police again. Tell them these two have shot up the place. Killed my husband and the others, but you've got them at gun point."

He nodded, handed the gun to her, and started walking to the phone. Before he was two steps into the journey, Margo raised the weapon and put a bullet through his skull. He dropped to the floor in front of us.

Fumbling with the gun in one hand and her clutch in the other, she managed to pull out a crisp white handkerchief. Tucking the clutch under her arm, she wiped the gun clean and explained herself.

"The silly lunk thought I loved him too. Ha! Thing is, if Miss Eva had shown up, I planned on giving her the penny. The man who gave it to me also gave me some advice. Seems you have to keep it hidden. Otherwise the demons will chase you down. All I wanted was enough money to be happy for the rest of my life. I got that now, don't I? She can have the penny, but of course I wouldn't give her the warning. I think she deserves a demonic visit. Hard-assed witch."

"And us?" Wolf asked.

"The doorman and girls at the hotel will tell the truth. You were working for a client that wanted something you thought I had. You showed up at the party, shot up the place trying to get to me, then followed me home and killed everyone here when you couldn't find your precious coin."

She looked at the dead bodyguard. "And you shot everyone in the back like cowards. Chances are you'll both get the chair, so I never have to deal with you again. No one's gonna believe you. No one's gonna take the word of couple of thugs like you over the grieving widow of Bernard Bentington."

Margo suddenly tossed the gun to me. Out of reflex, I caught it.

"And now your fingerprints are all over the murder weapon. You won't kill me, because you're really not that kind of man, are you? And if you are, you'll never find the penny."

I tilted my head as the sirens grew loud and flashing red lights appeared through the windows. "And you came up with this plan, on the spot?"

She shrugged. "Call me lucky, I guess."

"If you two run out the back, chances are that you'll get away. Oh, you'll be fugitives, but it's your only option for freedom," she smiled.

"Run? That'd be convenient for you, wouldn't it? A pair of thugs break in, steal a valuable coin, and kill everyone but you. Who'd doubt your story? But, if we stay and talk to the police... you know, tell them our side of the story... that could cause a problem for you, assuming your luck doesn't hold up."

Her eyes narrowed. "You and I know my luck is bulletproof."

Knowing I needed to do something before the cops stormed the place and started shooting, I stood and walked to the door, placing the pistol on the table beside the phone. I turned to Wolf and gave him a defeated look.

"Stay here. Chances are, they'll shoot first if they see you."

I heard the commotion of cars and men outside. Now, I prayed that my plan had worked.

Ten minutes later, a dozen police officers were in the house. Wolf and I sat on the stairs, wearing tightly locked handcuffs. Knowing better than to start anything, we took our seats and watched as one blue uniformed officer after another paraded through the front door, acting as if they owned the place.

The lead officer, Detective Hood, had been nice enough to keep his boys from bashing our faces in. Word had apparently gotten out about the events at the party, descriptions of us, and that we were armed and dangerous. The one officer standing guard, his gun nervously waving in my direction, never looked away, as if wanting an excuse to pull the trigger.

Startled, I jerked to the side, as an invisible hand snaked into my pants pocket, dangerously close to my manhood. A warm breath tickled my ear.

"Done," Luna said.

As quietly as I could, I asked. "How long?"

"How long what?" asked the officer.

Luna's breath rustled the hairs on the back of my neck, and I fought to keep from smiling.

I looked at the gun and then the officer. "Just talking to myself. Are you always this jumpy or did you have a bit too much coffee earlier?"

He ignored me and leaned back against the wall, looking at his boss instead of me.

Luna seized the opportunity. "It was right where you said it'd be. In the Bible, left on top of a couple of other books in her room. I had it in my hand when you came through the door."

I gave a subtle nod of appreciation and switched my focus to Detective Hood as he spoke on the phone.

"Thank you, ma'am. You've been most helpful. I'll have someone right over to look over the notes you made and take an official statement." Detective Hood looked at me through narrowed eyes as he replaced the receiver. He waved to the officer standing guard.

"Get the cuffs off them, and give'em back their guns."

The young man's eyes popped open. "Sir?"

"Just do it. And for goodness sake, put away your piece." Hood shook his head.

I watched as he stepped into the living room, where a crying Margo knelt beside her dead husband, holding him in her arms.

"Margo Bentington. You're under arrest for murder and conspiracy."

"Wh… what?"

Her tears continued to flow, but they became genuine as she was led out to a waiting car. The hateful side glance she threw at Wolf and I was priceless.

"The telephone operator corroborated your story. She overheard Mrs. Bentington's entire conversation with you gents. And she heard the gunshot and the stuff about the guard. That was a smart move." The officer nodded to the door. "We'll need official statements, but then you'll be free to go."

"There is one more thing, officer," I said, and filled him in on some juicy information.

The detective smiled. "I'll send a car."

Glancing at my watch, I looked to Wolf.

"We're cutting this close."

Nineteen

Parking the Studebaker, I ran from the garage to the front entrance to the Hotel Tennessee, stopping just short of the door. The scene looked pretty chaotic. Police cars sat everywhere, washing the buildings and bystanders with their flashing red lights.

Reporters and photographers clamored for spots close enough to shout questions at the police and their prisoner, a white-suited Cuban. Carlos left the building, struggling against the arresting officers. Spotting me as he reached the car, he stopped and yelled out something I didn't understand.

"I never could understand whatever gibberish they speak on that Godforsaken island he's from. But I think the gist of it that he'll kill you when he gets out." The familiar voice came from behind me.

I turned to face her. "No, Eva. I don't think he will."

The woman's face showed no emotion or indication of what she thought about the night's events. The evening air had a chill to it and I saw her lips tremble.

"Was he alone?" I asked, checking my watch.

She sighed. Her hand rose, clutching a small automatic pistol. "Yes. He is all I have left, aside from the few assigned to the club this evening."

"Too bad for you." I took another look at my watch, feeling anxious. I had fifteen minutes till midnight.

"I'll have him out by morning." Her voice sounded confident and calm.

I shook my head and pulled a cigarette from my jacket pocket. I offered her one. Smugly, she took it and the match I offered up.

"Don't think I won't use this," she said through a thin cloud of smoke.

"The police know your men were shooting up the party. Those Tommy's they used sprayed out a lot of lead, and a lot of innocent folks got hit. With all the press, the city leaders, and whatnot who saw everything, your boy going to be looking at a long stint in the slammer. They may even come after you."

I pointed to the pistol with my cigarette. "No silencer, and there are cops all about. Shoot me and they'll have you on murder in the first degree."

Miss Eva glanced around and slowly lowered the weapon.

"How did you know we'd be here?" she said, letting the smoke roll from her lips.

"Barkley. He told everyone to meet him at the bar." I checked my watch again, seeing that I only had twelve minutes remaining.

"You have the penny?" she asked, and I nodded.

She grunted. "Where are your friends?"

"Nowhere to be seen apparently. They offered the penny to me. Seems they felt my reason for chasing down the coin was more important than theirs."

Plucking the cigarette from her perfectly painted lips, she looked me up and down again. Smacking her lips, she flicked it away into the gutter.

I tapped my watch in front of her. "If you don't mind, I really gotta go."

"Doing it for your dame? Honorable, I guess. Leaving Memphis soon?" she said as I started walking towards the door.

I blew out a cloud of smoke and looked over my shoulder. "Driving out in the morning."

Her lips twitched and formed a halfhearted grin. "Make sure you do."

"Worried about your business?" I asked and watched as the first of the police cars began to pull away.

"No. The Rhino will weather this storm. My soul and my daughter…" the word lingered in the air as she looked to the sky.

"Ginger. You know she's dead, right? I saw you push her out of that elevator. There was room, but you wanted it for yourself and your man." My words dripped with hatred.

Her eyes moistened for the first time, and she looked at her feet. "I hadn't heard from her but hoped for the best."

I stopped and spun around, "Your daughter is one thing. Let's not forget your soul? It's not just the deal with Barkley you need to worry about. You have Ginger's blood on your hands too."

"Blood washes off, Mr. Dietrich. If she were the first to die because of me, I might be concerned, but in my line of business, death and killing is an occupational hazard. And Barkley seems like the gambling, bargaining type. I'll regain everything lost this evening."

"I know you will. Good night, Miss Eva."

She gave me a slow nod. "Good night, Mr. Dietrich. Do us both a favor. Don't come back to Memphis."

Sprinting away from Miss Eva, I charged through the lobby and entered the hotel's bar. Only a handful of patrons sat, consoling their troubles with spirits and bad company. In the same seat at the bar, Barkley sat, his back to me. He straightened a little as I stepped through the doorway, indicating he knew I had arrived.

Without looking back, he extended an arm, holding out his open hand and awaiting my offering.

"I knew of all of you, it'd be my boy Thomas who'd return what was lost."

I needed this to work, to be done with. I needed Natalie to be safe and awake. I pulled the penny from my pocket and looked at it. In my head, I repeated a phrase a few times.

Penny, you belong to me. Give me that good luck.

Holding on to the edge of the coin, I held it over Barkley's hand. Then I felt a slight tug on it.

"I know there must be temptation. Hanging on to all that luck for yourself. I wouldn't be surprised if you did want to keep it. In your line of work, an extra bit of luck could mean the difference between life and death for you and those around you. But let's face it, my boy. You're not built that way, are you? Go on. Drop it, Thomas and your lovely goes free."

I took a deep breath and counted down aloud.

"3…2…1."

My fingers opened, and I watched the penny drop. It fell into Barkley's open hand, which immediately closed around it. In the same instant, Luna appeared beside me, with Wolf beside her. She held onto him with one hand, their free fingers posed next to mine.

"You said whoever handed you the coin won. We all held it, so…"

I waited for him to protest. When nothing came from it, I continued.

"We all win."

Barkley spun on his stool, holding the penny between his fingers. He looked like a child on Christmas morning, grinning from ear to ear.

"I said…" I started.

He waved his free hand, as if shooing away a pesky fly. "Yes, yes. You all won. None of that matters."

"What do you mean none of that matters?" Wolf demanded.

Barkley looked at him, and then at all of us. "This wasn't about collecting souls. It was about retrieving the coin. Any souls I gained for my Master in the process were… what do you call it? Gravy? In any case, my boy, you've done it. You all did."

"So, my mother?" Luna asked.

"My minions will alter the police file to ensure

her safety. Wolf, your client's son is off the hook. And you, Thomas, Natalie will wake up as soon as you get to your room. Her soul is clean and mortgage-free." He chuckled and winked as he stood, walking to the door. With a glance back at us, he waved and disappeared.

Wolf echoed what we all were thinking. "We won. It's over."

"Whiskey," Luna said loudly to the bartender and looked at Wolf and me. "Three of them and make them doubles. Ya know what, just leave the damn bottle."

I shook my head. "No thanks. I gotta get upstairs."

"Dietrich!" Luna shouted at my back as I was halfway to the door. Looking back, she continued. "Breakfast, tomorrow morning…"

"Say ten at our favorite diner," Wolf chimed in.

Running from the elevator, I opened the hotel door and peered in on the sleeping woman. Tossing my torn, scorched, and blood-splattered jacket over the chair as I charged across the room, I sat beside her. She didn't move, and my heart skipped a beat.

I leaned in and kissed her bare shoulder. Stirring, eyelids fluttered then opened, revealing her beautiful eyes.

"What—what time is it?" she asked in a sleepy tone.

"A bit after midnight. You've been asleep for a while."

She slowly sat up, blinking. Looking around, her eyes eventually focused on me.

"Where is... what was her name? The hottie?" She rubbed her eyes. "Wait. Did you say midnight? We didn't get back to the room until three-something."

I started to explain, but she held up a finger to my bruised and split lip.

"Were you in a fight?"

"Something like that." I stretched, popping my back and neck.

Blinking hard, she looked me over. Blood still seeped from the cuts on my chest, arms, and my left hand. She reached up and ran her hands along my bruised jaw, making me flinch a couple of times.

"What the hell happened to you?" she asked and immediately reached for the phone on the nightstand.

"Who are you calling?" I asked.

A short time late, room service delivered hamburgers for the two of us, as well as the hotel's first aid kit. For the next hour, Natalie cleaned and bandaged my cuts and scrapes. Growing up on a farm, she had a knack for stitching up wounds on the farm animals, as well as closing up my sliced up hand and chest.

As she ate and doctored, I filled her in on the day's events, along with the deal that'd transpired in the bar, the night before.

"All I remember about last night was the hottie and the recording deal." She sat back, looking down and frowning. "I shouldn't be disappointed. I mean, I got duped, we both did. But I really wanted that part of it to be real."

"I love you, kitten," I whispered as I kissed her hand. "When we get back to Nashville, we'll figure out a way to make your dream come true."

We laid down and, in no time, were fast asleep.

The next morning, we left the hotel behind and walked to the diner. Luna and Wolf already had a booth and four cups of steaming hot coffee on the table. Introductions were made, and we joked about how the day would be boring compared to yesterday.

"Thomas told me that you were willing to give him the penny. Thank you," Natalie said.

They nodded, and I echoed Natalie's sentiment.

"Continuing the vacation?" Luna asked.

I said yes while Natalie said no. We looked at one another.

"Sweet pea," Natalie said, and tapped on the Rolex on my wrist. "I think you spent most of our vacation money on that." She tugged my sleeve up a bit and eyed the watch. "But it does look good on you."

"What about you two?" I asked, looking back and forth between Luna and Wolf.

"I'm heading out as soon as we're done here. I need to let my client know his son has his soul again," Wolf said.

Luna looked at me with a coy smile. "I'm going back home too. After watching you two work, I think a change is in order."

"What kind of change?" Wolf asked.

"Now that I know that my soul is a real thing and, you know, that there really is a Heaven and Hell, I need to make some changes in my life. Time to turn over a new leaf. Instead of being a thief, I'm serious about using my talents as a Private Investigator."

Smiling, I said, "I think you'll make a damn good one."

We ate and talked before stepping out of the diner. Phone numbers and addresses were exchanged, as well as promises to stay in touch. My unlikely partners had become close friends over the course of a day.

Natalie and I held hands as we walked to the

parking garage.

"I'm sorry," I whispered.

"Sorry? About what?"

I looked into her eyes. "I blew too much money of our vacation money."

She laughed. "Sweet pea think of it as a business expense, all used to win my soul back. We can always go on a trip next year. What matters to me is…"

I opened the car door for her and watched as she slid inside. Looking up at me, she continued. "What matters to me is that I'm with you."

Leaning over, I kissed her. "Miss Knight, I don't deserve you."

Natalie smiled and winked. "Mr. Dietrich, I know that."

Getting into the car, we laughed and headed for home.

The world of Thomas Dietrich is about to get bigger. Keep reading and explore the dark, seedy side of America's Music City.

Voodoo Rumors – 1951

The Blood Red Ruby – available now

The Last Encore – available now

A Penny for Luck – available now

Wild Pooch – coming August 2018

Doomsday, The Devil, and a girl named Betty – coming October 2018

Dietrich's Inferno – Coming December 2018

Keep up with Thomas Dietrich at

www.voodoorumors.com

About the Author

Chattanooga native, D. Alan Lewis's debut novel, *The Blood in Snowflake Garden* was a finalist for the 2010 Claymore Award. Alan's other novels include, *The Lightning Bolts of Zeus, Keely,* and *The Bishop of Port Victoria*. He is the editor of four anthologies from Dark Oak Press, *Capes & Clockwork 1 & 2* and the 2 *Luna's Children* volumes. Alan has numerous short stories published and has won multiple awards for his steampunk short stories and novellas. He is a frequent speaker/guest at various genre conventions and runs writing & publishing workshops.

You can follow Alan at his website: **www.dalanlewis.com** Or on Facebook: **Author-D-Alan-Lewis** Or on Twitter: @Dalanlewis

Check out the latest on Voodoo Rumors at **www.voodoorumors.com**.

GUNFIGHTS, AIRSHIPS AND BULLET-PROOF CORSETS ARE JUST PART OF THE JOB FOR AMERICA'S PREMIERE STEAMPUNK SPIES.

Hawke Girls

THE LIGHTNING BOLTS OF ZEUS

BOOK 1 OF THE HAWKE GIRLS' ADVENTURES

BY D. ALAN LEWIS

AVAILABLE ON AMAZON.COM OR YOUR LOCAL BOOK SELLER.

Made in the USA
Monee, IL
21 November 2021

82439914R00144